FIRE-T

Sir Charles said, "I believe
"You mean that there is so
"I do."

"H'm," said Harley. "Even if the facts are ...., ou have fairly substantial grounds for such a suspicion?"

"I cannot say that they are substantial, Mr. Harley. They are rather more circumstantial. You are naturally anxious for the particulars. They bear, I regret to say, a close resemblance to the symptoms of a well-known form of hallucination. In short, with one exception, they may practically all be classed under the head of surveillance."

"Surveillance," said Paul Harley. "You mean that you are more or less constantly followed?"

"I do."

"And what is your impression of this follower?"

"A very hazy one. Tonight, as I came to your office, I have every reason to believe that someone followed me in a taxicab."

"Anything else?"

"One very notable thing, Mr. Harley. I was actually assaulted less than a week ago within sight of my own house. I had been to visit a friend in the neighbourhood, whom I am at present attending professionally, although I am actually retired. I was returning across the square, close to midnight, when, fortunately for myself, I detected the sound of light, pattering footsteps immediately behind me. The place was quite deserted at that hour, and although I was so near home, the worst would have happened, I fear, if my sense of hearing had been less acute. I turned in the very instant that a man was about to spring upon me from behind. He was holding in his hand what looked like a large silk handkerchief. This encounter took place in the shadow of some trees, and beyond the fact that my assailant was a small man, I could form no impression of his identity."

"What did you do?"

"I turned and struck out with my stick."

"And then?"

"Then he made no attempt to contest the issue, but simply ran swiftly off, always keeping in the shadows of the trees."

"H'm," mused Harley. "A very alarming occurrence, Sir Charles. It must have shaken you very badly. But we must not overlook the possibility that this may have been an ordinary footpad."

"His methods were scarcely those of a footpad," murmured Sir Charles.

"I quite agree," said Harley. "They were rather Oriental, if I may say so."

ALSO BY SAX ROHMER
Dope
The Golden Scorpion
The Green Eyes of Bast
The Return of Fu Manchu
The Hand of Fu Manchu
The Yellow Claw

BY H. RIDER HAGGARD
Allan Quatermain and the Ice Gods
Allan Quatermain's Wife
Allan and the Holy Flower
The Ancient Allan
Belshazzar
Child of Storm
Cleopatra
Colonel Quaritch, V.C.
Eric Brighteyes
Heu-Heu or the Monster
The Ivory Child
Jess
Margaret
Marie
Montezuma's Daughter
Moon of Israel: A Tale of the Exodus
Mr. Meeson's Will
Nada the Lily
Pearl-Maiden
Queen of the Dawn
Regeneration
She and Allan
The Spirit of Bambatse
Swallow: A Tale of the Great Trek
The Virgin of the Sun
The Wanderer's Necklace
The Witch's Head
The World's Desire
The Yellow God: An Idol of Africa

FIRE-TONGUE

SAX ROHMER

WILDSIDE PRESS

FIRE-TONGUE

Published by
Wildside Press
P. O. Box 301
Holicong, PA 18928-0301
www.wildsidepress.com

Copyright © 2002 by Wildside Press
All Rights Reserved.

I

A CLIENT FOR PAUL HARLEY

SOME OF PAUL HARLEY'S most interesting cases were brought to his notice in an almost accidental way. Although he closed his office in Chancery Lane sharply at the hour of six, the hour of six by no means marked the end of his business day. His work was practically ceaseless. But even in times of leisure, at the club or theatre, fate would sometimes cast in his path the first slender thread which was ultimately to lead him into some unsuspected labyrinth, perhaps in the underworld of London, perhaps in a city of the Far East.

His investigation of the case of the man with the shaven skull afforded an instance of this, and even more notable was his first meeting with Major Jack Ragstaff of the Cavalry Club, a meeting which took place after the office had been closed, but which led to the unmasking of perhaps the most cunning murderer in the annals of crime.

One summer's evening when the little clock upon his table was rapidly approaching the much-desired hour, Harley lay back in his chair and stared meditatively across his private office in the direction of a large and very handsome Burmese cabinet, which seemed strangely out of place amid the filing drawers, bookshelves, and other usual impedimenta of a professional man. A peculiarly uninteresting week was drawing to a close, and he was wondering if this betokened a decreased activity in the higher criminal circles, or whether it was merely one of those usual quiescent periods which characterize every form of warfare.

Paul Harley, although the fact was unknown to the general public, occupied something of the position of an unofficial field marshal of the forces arrayed against evildoers. Throughout the war he had undertaken confidential work of the highest importance, especially in regard to the Near East, with which he was intimately acquainted. A member of the English bar, and the last court of appeal to which Home Office and Foreign Office alike came in troubled times, the brass plate upon the door of his unassuming premises in Chancery Lane conveyed little or nothing to the uninitiated.

The man himself, with his tropical bronze and air of eager vitality, must have told the most careless observer that he stood in the presence of an extraordinary personality. He was slightly gray at the temples in these days, but young in mind and body, physically fit, and possessed of an intellectual keenness which had forced recognition from two hemispheres. His office was part of an old city residence, and his chambers adjoined his workroom, so that now, noting that his table clock registered the hour of six, he pressed a bell which summoned Innes, his confidential secretary.

"Well, Innes," said Harley, looking around, "another uneventful day."

"Very uneventful, Mr. Harley. About a month of this and you will have to resume practice at the bar."

Paul Harley laughed.

"Not a bit likely, Innes," he replied. "No more briefs for me. I shall retire to Norfolk and devote my declining years to fishing."

"I don't know that fishing would entirely satisfy me," said Innes.

"It would more than satisfy me," returned Harley. "But every man to his own ambition. Well, there is no occasion to wait; you might as well get along. But what's that you've got in your hand?"

"Well," replied Innes, laying a card upon the table, "I was just coming in with it when you rang."

Paul Harley glanced at the card.

"Sir Charles Abingdon," he read aloud, staring reflectively at his secretary. "That is the osteologist?"

"Yes," answered Innes, "but I fancy he has retired from practice."

"Ah," murmured Harley, "I wonder what he wants. I suppose I had better see him, as I fancy that he and I met casually some years ago in India. Ask him to come in, will you?"

Innes retired, and there presently entered a distinguished-looking, elderly gentleman upon whose florid face rested an expression not unlike that of embarrassment.

"Mr. Harley," he began, "I feel somewhat ill at ease in encroaching upon your time, for I am by no means sure that my case comes within your particular province."

"Sit down, Sir Charles," said Harley with quiet geniality. "Officially, my working day is ended; but if nothing comes of your visit beyond a chat it will have been very welcome. Calcutta, was it not, where we last met?"

"It was," replied Sir Charles, placing his hat and cane upon the table and sitting down rather wearily in a big leather armchair which Harley had pushed forward. "If I presume upon so slight an acquaintance, I am sorry, but I must confess that only the fact of having met you socially encouraged me to make this visit."

He raised his eyes to Harley's face and gazed at him with that peculiarly searching look which belongs to members of his profession, but mingled with it was an expression of almost pathetic appeal, of appeal for understanding, for sympathy of some kind.

"Go on, Sir Charles," said Harley. He pushed forward a box of cigars. "Will you smoke?"

"Thanks, no," was the answer.

Sir Charles evidently was oppressed by some secret trouble, thus

Harley mused silently, as, taking out a tin of tobacco from a cabinet beside him, he began in leisurely manner to load a briar. In this he desired to convey that he treated the visit as that of a friend, and also, since business was over, that Sir Charles might without scruple speak at length and at leisure of whatever matters had brought him there.

"Very well, then," began the surgeon. "I am painfully conscious that the facts which I am in a position to lay before you are very scanty and unsatisfactory."

Paul Harley nodded encouragingly. "If this were not so," he explained, "you would have no occasion to apply to me, Sir Charles. It is my business to look for facts. Naturally, I do not expect my clients to supply them."

Sir Charles slowly nodded his head, and seemed in some measure to recover confidence.

"Briefly, then," he said, "I believe my life is in danger."

"You mean that there is someone who desires your death?"

"I do."

"H'm," said Harley, replacing the tin in the cupboard and striking a match. "Even if the facts are scanty, no doubt you have fairly substantial grounds for such a suspicion?"

"I cannot say that they are substantial, Mr. Harley. They are rather more circumstantial. Frankly, I have forced myself to come here, and now that I have intruded upon your privacy, I realize my difficulties more keenly than ever."

The expression of embarrassment upon the speaker's face had grown intense, and now he paused, bending forward in his chair. He seemed in his glance to appeal for patience on the part of his hearer, and Harley, lighting his pipe, nodded in understanding fashion. He was the last man in the world to jump to conclusions. He had learned by bitter experience that lightly to dismiss such cases as this of Sir Charles as coming within the province of delusion, was sometimes tantamount to refusing aid to a man in deadly peril.

"You are naturally anxious for the particulars," Sir Charles presently resumed. "They bear, I regret to say, a close resemblance to the symptoms of a well-known form of hallucination. In short, with one exception, they may practically all be classed under the head of surveillance."

"Surveillance," said Paul Harley. "You mean that you are more or less constantly followed?"

"I do."

"And what is your impression of this follower?"

"A very hazy one. Tonight, as I came to your office, I have every reason to believe that someone followed me in a taxicab."

"You came in a car?"

"I did."

"And a cab followed you the whole way?"

"Practically the whole way, except that as my chauffeur turned into Chancery Lane, the cab stopped at the corner of Fleet Street."

"Your idea is that your pursuer followed on foot from this point?"

"Such was my impression."

"H'm, quite impossible. And is this sort of thing constant, Sir Charles?"

"It has been for some time past."

"Anything else?"

"One very notable thing, Mr. Harley. I was actually assaulted less than a week ago within sight of my own house."

"Indeed! Tell me of this." Paul Harley became aware of an awakening curiosity. Sir Charles Abingdon was not the type of man who is lightly intimidated.

"I had been to visit a friend in the neighbourhood," Sir Charles continued, "whom I am at present attending professionally, although I am actually retired. I was returning across the square, close to midnight, when, fortunately for myself, I detected the sound of light, pattering footsteps immediately behind me. The place was quite deserted at that hour, and although I was so near home, the worst would have happened, I fear, if my sense of hearing had been less acute. I turned in the very instant that a man was about to spring upon me from behind. He was holding in his hand what looked like a large silk handkerchief. This encounter took place in the shadow of some trees, and beyond the fact that my assailant was a small man, I could form no impression of his identity."

"What did you do?"

"I turned and struck out with my stick."

"And then?"

"Then he made no attempt to contest the issue, but simply ran swiftly off, always keeping in the shadows of the trees."

"Very strange," murmured Harley. "Do you think he had meant to drug you?"

"Maybe," replied Sir Charles. "The handkerchief was perhaps saturated with some drug, or he may even have designed to attempt to strangle me."

"And you formed absolutely no impression of the man?"

"None whatever, Mr. Harley. When you see the spot at which the encounter took place, if you care to do so, you will recognize the difficulties. It is perfectly dark there after nightfall."

"H'm," mused Harley. "A very alarming occurrence, Sir Charles. It must have shaken you very badly. But we must not overlook the possibility that this may have been an ordinary footpad."

"His methods were scarcely those of a footpad," murmured Sir Charles.

"I quite agree," said Harley. "They were rather Oriental, if I may say so."

Sir Charles Abingdon started. "Oriental!" he whispered. "Yes, you are right."

"Does this suggest a train of thought?" prompted Harley.

Sir Charles Abingdon cleared his throat nervously. "It does, Mr. Harley," he admitted, "but a very confusing one. It leads me to a point which I must mention, but which concerns a very well-known man. Before I proceed I should like to make it clear that I do not believe for a moment that he is responsible for this unpleasant business."

Harley stared at him curiously. "Nevertheless," he said, "there must be some data in your possession which suggest to your mind that he has some connection with it."

"There are, Mr. Harley, and I should be deeply indebted if you could visit my house this evening, when I could place this evidence, if evidence it may be called, before you. I find myself in so delicate a position. If you are free I should welcome your company at dinner."

Paul Harley seemed to be reflecting.

"Of course, Sir Charles," he said, presently, "your statement is very interesting and curious, and I shall naturally make a point of going fully into the matter. But before proceeding further there are two questions I should like to ask you. The first is this: What is the name of the 'well-known' man to whom you refer? And the second: If not he then whom do you suspect of being behind all this?"

"The one matter is so hopelessly involved in the other," he finally replied, "that although I came here prepared as I thought with a full statement of the case, I should welcome a further opportunity of rearranging the facts before imparting them to you. One thing, however, I have omitted to mention. It is, perhaps, of paramount importance. There was a robbery at my house less than a week ago."

"What! A robbery! Tell me: what was stolen?"

"Nothing of the slightest value, Mr. Harley, to any one but myself—or so I should have supposed." The speaker coughed nervously. "The thief had gained admittance to my private study, where there are several cases of Oriental jewelry and a number of pieces of valuable gold and silverware, all antique. At what hour he came, how he gained admittance, and how he retired, I cannot imagine. All the doors were locked as usual in the morning and nothing was disturbed."

"I don't understand, then."

"I chanced to have occasion to open my bureau which I invariably keep locked. Immediately—immediately—I perceived that my papers were disarranged. Close examination revealed the fact that a short manuscript in my own hand, which had been placed in one of the pigeonholes, was missing."

"A manuscript," murmured Harley. "Upon a technical subject?"

"Scarcely a technical subject, Mr. Harley. It was a brief account which I had vaguely contemplated publishing in one of the reviews, a brief account of a very extraordinary patient whom I once attended."

"And had you written it recently?"

"No; some years ago. But I had recently added to it. I may say that it was my purpose still further to add to it, and with this object I had actually unlocked the bureau."

"New facts respecting this patient had come into your possession?"

"They had."

"Before the date of the attack upon you?"

"Before that date, yes."

"And before surveillance of your movements began?"

"I believe so."

"May I suggest that your patient and the 'well-known man' to whom you referred are one and the same?"

"It is not so, Mr. Harley," returned Sir Charles in a tired voice. "Nothing so simple. I realize more than ever that I must arrange my facts in some sort of historical order. Therefore I ask you again: will you dine with me tonight?"

"With pleasure," replied Harley, promptly. "I have no other engagement."

That his ready acceptance had immensely relieved the troubled mind of Sir Charles was evident enough. His visitor stood up. "I am not prone to sickly fancies, Mr. Harley," he said. "But a conviction has been growing upon me for some time that I have incurred, how I cannot imagine, but that nevertheless I have incurred powerful enmity. I trust our evening's counsel may enable you, with your highly specialized faculties, to detect an explanation."

And it was instructive to note how fluently he spoke now that he found himself temporarily relieved of the necessity of confessing the source of his mysterious fears.

II

THE SIXTH SENSE

PAUL HARLEY STEPPED into his car in Chancery Lane. "Drive in the direction of Hyde Park Corner," he directed the chauffeur. "Go along the Strand."

Glancing neither right nor left, he entered the car, and presently they were proceeding slowly with the stream of traffic in the Strand. "Pull up at the Savoy," he said suddenly through the tube.

The car slowed down in that little bay which contains the entrance to the hotel, and Harley stared fixedly out of the rear window, observing the occupants of all other cars and cabs which were following. For three minutes or more he remained there watching. "Go on," he directed.

Again they proceeded westward and, half-way along Piccadilly, "Stop at the Ritz," came the order.

The car pulled up before the colonnade and Harley, stepping out, dismissed the man and entered the hotel, walked through to the side entrance, and directed a porter to get him a taxicab. In this he proceeded to the house of Sir Charles Abingdon. He had been seeking to learn whether he was followed, but in none of the faces he had scrutinized had he detected any interest in himself, so that his idea that whoever was watching Sir Charles in all probability would have transferred attention to himself remained no more than an idea. For all he had gained by his tactics, Sir Charles's theory might be no more than a delusion after all.

The house of Sir Charles Abingdon was one of those small, discreet establishments, the very neatness of whose appointments inspires respect for the occupant. If anything had occurred during the journey to suggest to Harley that Sir Charles was indeed under observation by a hidden enemy, the suave British security and prosperity of his residence must have destroyed the impression.

As the cab was driven away around the corner, Harley paused for a moment, glancing about him to right and left and up at the neatly curtained windows. In the interval which had elapsed since Sir Charles's departure from his office, he had had leisure to survey the outstanding features of the story, and, discounting in his absence the pathetic sincerity of the narrator, he had formed the opinion that there was nothing in the account which was not susceptible of an ordinary prosaic explanation.

Sir Charles's hesitancy in regard to two of the questions asked had contained a hint that they might involve intimate personal matters, and Harley was prepared to learn that the source of the distinguished surgeon's dread lay in some unrevealed episode of the past. Beyond the fact that Sir Charles was a widower, he knew little or nothing of his private life. He was far too experienced an investigator to formulate theories until all the facts were in his possession. Therefore it was with keen interest that he looked forward to the interview.

Familiarity with crime, in its many complexions, East and West, had developed in Paul Harley a sort of sixth sense. It was an evasive, fickle thing, but was nevertheless the attribute which had made him an investigator of genius. Often enough it failed him entirely. It had failed him tonight—or else no one had followed him from Chancery Lane.

It had failed him earlier in the evening when, secretly, he had watched from the office window Sir Charles's car proceeding toward the Strand. That odd, sudden chill, as of an abrupt lowering of the temperature, which often advised him of the nearness of malignant activity, had not been experienced.

Now, standing before Sir Charles's house, he "sensed" the atmosphere keenly—seeking for the note of danger.

There had been a thunder shower just before he had set out, and now, although rain had ceased, the sky remained blackly overcast and a curious, dull stillness was come. The air had a welcome freshness and the glistening pavements looked delightfully cool after the parching heat of the day. In the quiet square, no doubt, it was always restful in contrast with the more busy highroads, and in the murmur of distant traffic he found something very soothing. About him then were peace, prosperity, and security.

Yet, as he stood there, waiting—it came to him: the note of danger. Swiftly he looked to right and left, trying to penetrate the premature dusk. The whole complexion of the matter changed. Some menace intangible now, but which at any moment might become evident—lay near him. It was sheer intuition, no doubt, but it convinced him.

A moment later he had rung the bell, and as a man opened the door, showing a easy and well-lighted lobby within, the fear aura no longer touched Paul Harley. Out from the doorway came hominess and that air of security and peace which had seemed to characterize the house when viewed from outside. The focus of menace, therefore, lay not inside the house of Sir Charles but without. It was very curious. In the next instant came a possible explanation.

"Mr. Paul Harley?" said the butler tentatively.

"Yes, I am he."

"Sir Charles is expecting you, sir. He apologizes for not being in to receive you. but he will only be absent a few minutes."

"Sir Charles has been called out?" inquired Harley as he handed hat and coat to the man.

"Yes, sir. He is attending Mr. Chester Wilson on the other side of the square, and Mr. Wilson's man rang up a few moments ago requesting Sir Charles to step across."

"I see," murmured Harley, as the butler showed him into a small but well-filled library on the left of the lobby.

Refreshments were set invitingly upon a table beside a deep lounge chair. But Harley declined the man's request to refresh himself while waiting and began aimlessly to wander about the room, apparently studying the titles of the works crowding the bookshelves. As a matter of fact, he was endeavouring to arrange certain ideas in order, and if he had been questioned on the subject it is improbable that he could have mentioned the title of one book in the library.

His mental equipment was of a character too rarely met with in the profession to which he belonged. While up to the very moment of reaching Sir Charles's house he had doubted the reality of the menace which hung over this man, the note of danger which he had sensed at the very threshold had convinced him, where more ordinary circumstantial evidence might have left him in doubt.

It was perhaps pure imagination, but experience had taught him that it was closely allied to clairvoyance.

Now upon his musing there suddenly intruded sounds of a muffled altercation. That is to say, the speakers, who were evidently in the lobby beyond the library door, spoke in low tones, perhaps in deference to the presence of a visitor. Harley was only mildly interested, but the voices had broken his train of thought, and when presently the door opened to admit a very neat but rather grim-looking old lady he started, then looked across at her with a smile.

Some of the grimness faded from the wrinkled old face, and the housekeeper, for this her appearance proclaimed her to be, bowed in a queer Victorian fashion which suggested that a curtsy might follow. One did not follow, however. "I am sure I apologize, sir," she said. "Benson did not tell me you had arrived."

"That's quite all right," said Harley, genially.

His smile held a hint of amusement, for in the comprehensive glance which the old lady cast across the library, a glance keen to detect disorder and from which no speck of dust could hope to conceal itself, there remained a trace of that grimness which he had detected at the moment of her entrance. In short, she was still bristling from a recent encounter. So much so that detecting something sympathetic in Harley's smile she availed herself of the presence of a badly arranged vase of flowers to linger and to air her grievances.

"Servants in these times," she informed him, her fingers busily rearranging the blooms, "are not what servants were in my young days."

"Unfortunately, that is so," Harley agreed.

The old lady tossed her head. "I do my best," she continued, "but that girl would not have stayed in the house for one week if I had had my way. Miss Phil is altogether too soft-hearted. Thank goodness, she goes tomorrow, though."

"You don't refer to Miss Phil?" said Harley, intentionally misunderstanding.

"Gracious goodness, no!" exclaimed the house keeper, and laughed with simple glee at the joke. "I mean Jones, the new parlourmaid. When I say new, they are all new, for none of them stay longer than three months."

"Indeed," smiled Harley, who perceived that the old lady was something of a martinet.

"Indeed, they don't. Think they are ladies nowadays. Four hours off has that girl had today, although she was out on Wednesday. Then she has the impudence to allow someone to ring her up here at the house, and finally I discover her upsetting the table after Benson had laid it and after I had rearranged it."

She glanced indignantly in the direction of the lobby. "Perhaps one day," she concluded, pathetically, as she walked slowly from the room, "we shall find a parlourmaid who is a parlourmaid. Good evening, sir,"

"Good evening," said Harley, quietly amused to be made the recipient of these domestic confidences.

He continued to smile for some time after the door had been closed. His former train of ideas was utterly destroyed, but for this he was not ungrateful to the housekeeper, since the outstanding disadvantage of that strange gift resembling prescience was that it sometimes blunted the purely analytical part of his mind when this should have been at its keenest. He was now prepared to listen to what Sir Charles had to say and to judge impartially of its evidential value.

Wandering from side to side of the library, he presently found himself standing still before the mantelpiece and studying a photograph in a silver frame which occupied the centre of the shelf. It was the photograph of an unusually pretty girl; that is to say, of a girl whose beauty was undeniable, but who belonged to a type widely removed from that of the ordinary good-looking Englishwoman.

The outline of her face was soft and charming, and there was a questioning look in her eyes which was alluring and challenging. Her naive expression was palpably a pose, and her slightly parted lips promised laughter. She possessed delightfully wavy hair and her neck and one shoulder, which were bare, had a Grecian purity. Harley discovered himself to be smiling at the naive lady of the photograph.

"Presumably 'Miss Phil'," he said aloud.

He removed his gaze with reluctance from the fascinating picture, and dropping into the big lounge chair, he lighted a cigarette. He had just placed the match in an ash tray when he heard Sir Charles's voice in the lobby, and a moment later Sir Charles himself came hurrying into the library. His expression was so peculiar that Harley started up immediately, perceiving that something unusual had happened.

"My dear Mr. Harley," began Sir Charles, "in the first place pray accept my apologies—"

"None are necessary," Harley interrupted. "Your excellent housekeeper has entertained me vastly."

"Good, good," muttered Sir Charles. "I am obliged to Mrs. Howett," and it was plainly to be seen that his thoughts were elsewhere. "But I have to relate a most inexplicable occurrence—inexplicable unless by some divine accident the plan has been prevented from maturing."

"What do you mean, Sir Charles?"

"I was called ten minutes ago by someone purporting to be the servant of Mr. Chester Wilson, that friend and neighbour whom I have been attending."

"So your butler informed me."

"My dear sir," cried Sir Charles, and the expression in his eyes grew almost wild, "no one in Wilson's house knew anything about the matter!"

"What! It was a ruse?"

"Palpably a ruse to get me away from home."

Harley dropped his cigarette into the ash tray beside the match, where, smouldering, it sent up a gray spiral into the air of the library. Whether because of his words or because of the presence of the man himself, the warning, intuitive finger had again touched Paul Harley. "You saw or heard nothing on your way across the square to suggest that any one having designs on your safety was watching you?"

"Nothing. I searched the shadows most particularly on my return journey, of course. For the thing cannot have been purposeless."

"I quite agree with you," said Paul Harley, quietly.

Between the promptings of that uncanny sixth sense of his and the working of the trained deductive reasoning powers, he was momentarily at a loss. Some fact, some episode, a memory, was clamouring for recognition, while the intuitive, subconscious voice whispered: "This man is in danger; protect him." What was the meaning of it all? He felt that a clue lay somewhere outside the reach of his intelligence, and a sort of anger possessed him because of his impotence to grasp it.

Sir Charles was staring at him in that curiously pathetic way which he had observed at their earlier interview in Chancery Large. "In any event," said his host, "let us dine: for already I have kept you waiting."

Harley merely bowed, and walking out of the library, entered the cosy dining room. A dreadful premonition had claimed him as his glance had met that of Sir Charles—a premonition that this man's days were numbered. It was uncanny, unnerving; and whereas, at first, the atmosphere of Sir Charles Abingdon's home had been laden with prosperous security, now from every side, and even penetrating to the warmly lighted dining room, came that chilling note of danger.

In crossing the lobby he had not failed to note that there were many Indian curios in the place which could not well have failed to attract the attention of a burglar. But that the person who had penetrated to the house was no common burglar he was now assured and he required no further evidence upon this point.

As he took his seat at the dining table he observed that Sir Charles's collection had overflowed even into this room. In the warm shadows about him were pictures and ornaments, all of which came from, or had been inspired by, the Far East.

In this Oriental environment lay an inspiration. The terror which had come into Sir Charles's life, the invisible menace which, swordlike, hung over him, surely belonged in its eerie quality to the land of temple bells, of silent, subtle peoples, to the secret land which has bred so many mysteries. Yes, he must look into the past, into the Indian life of Sir Charles Abingdon, for the birth of this thing which now had grown into a shadow almost tangible.

Benson attended at table, assisted by a dark-faced and very surly-looking maid, in whom Harley thought he recognized the housekeeper's bete noire.

When presently both servants had temporarily retired. "You see, Mr. Harley," began Sir Charles, glancing about his own room in a manner almost furtive, "I realized today at your office that the history of this dread which has come upon me perhaps went back so far that it was almost impossible to acquaint you with it under the circumstances."

"I quite understand."

"I think perhaps I should inform you in the first place that I have a daughter. Her mother has been dead for many years, and perhaps I have not given her the attention which a motherless girl is entitled to expect from her father. I don't mean," he said, hastily, "that we are in any sense out of sympathy, but lately in some way I must confess that we have got a little out of touch." He glanced anxiously at his guest, indeed almost apologetically. "You will of course understand, Mr. Harley, that this seeming preamble may prove to have a direct bearing upon what I propose to tell you?"

"Pray tell the story in your own way, Sir Charles," said Harley with sympathy. "I am all attention, and I shall only interrupt you in the event of any point not being quite clear."

"Thank you," said Sir Charles. "I find it so much easier to explain the matter now. To continue, there is a certain distinguished Oriental gentleman "

He paused as Benson appeared to remove the soup plates.

"It is always delightful to chat with one who knows India so well as you do," he continued, glancing significantly at his guest.

Paul Harley, who fully appreciated the purpose of this abrupt change in the conversation, nodded in agreement. "The call of the East," he replied, "is a very real thing. Only one who has heard it can understand and appreciate all it means."

The butler, an excellently trained servant, went about his work with quiet efficiency, and once Harley heard him mutter rapid instructions to the surly parlourmaid, who hovered disdainfully in the background. When again host and guest found themselves alone: "I don't in any way distrust the servants," explained Sir Charles, "but one cannot hope to prevent gossip." He raised his serviette to his lips and almost immediately resumed: "I was about to tell you, Mr. Harley, about my daughter's—"

He paused and cleared his throat, then, hastily pouring out a glass of water, he drank a sip or two and Paul Harley noticed that his hand was shaking nervously. He thought of the photograph in the library, and now, in this reference to a distinguished Oriental gentleman, he suddenly perceived the possible drift of the conversation.

This was the point to which Sir Charles evidently experienced such difficulty in coming. It was something which concerned his daughter and, mentally visualizing the pure oval face and taunting eyes of the library photograph, Harley found it impossible to believe that the evil which threatened Sir Charles could possibly be associated in any way with Phyllis Abingdon.

Yet, if the revelation which he had to make must be held responsible for his present condition, then truly it was a dreadful one. No longer able to conceal his concern, Harley stood up. "If the story distresses you so keenly, Sir Charles," he said, "I beg—"

Sir Charles waved his hand reassuringly. "A mere nothing. It will pass," he whispered.

"But I fear," continued Harley, "that—"

He ceased abruptly, and ran to his host's assistance, for the latter, evidently enough, was in the throes of some sudden illness or seizure. His fresh-coloured face was growing positively livid, and he plucked at the edge of the table with twitching fingers. As Harley reached his side he made a sudden effort to stand up, throwing out his arm to grasp the other's shoulder.

"Benson!" cried Harley, loudly. "Quick! Your master is ill!"

There came a sound of swift footsteps and the door was thrown open.

"Too late," whispered Sir Charles in a choking voice. He began to clutch his throat as Benson hurried into the room.

"My God!" whispered Harley. "He is dying!"

Indeed, the truth was all too apparent. Sir Charles Abingdon was almost past speech. He was glaring across the table as though he saw some ghastly apparition there. And now with appalling suddenness he became as a dead weight in Harley's supporting grasp. Raspingly, as if forced in agony from his lips:

"Fire-Tongue . . ." he said. "Nicol Brinn . . ."

Benson, white and terror-stricken, bent over him.

"Sir Charles!" he kept muttering. "Sir Charles! What is the matter, sir?"

A stifled shriek sounded from the doorway, and in tottered Mrs. Howett, the old housekeeper, with other servants peering over her shoulder into that warmly lighted dining room where Sir Charles Abingdon lay huddled in his own chair—dead.

III

SHADOWS

"HAD YOU REASON to suspect any cardiac trouble, Doctor McMurdoch?" asked Harley.

Doctor McMurdoch, a local practitioner who had been a friend of Sir Charles Abingdon, shook his head slowly. He was a tall, preternaturally thin Scotsman, clean-shaven, with shaggy dark brows and a most gloomy expression in his deep-set eyes. While the presence of his sepulchral figure seemed appropriate enough in that stricken house, Harley could not help thinking that it must have been far from reassuring in a sick room.

"I had never actually detected anything of the kind," replied the physician, and his deep voice was gloomily in keeping with his personality. "I had observed a certain breathlessness at times, however. No doubt it is one of those cases of on suspected endocarditis. Acute. I take it," raising his shaggy brows interrogatively, "that nothing had occurred to excite Sir Charles?"

"On the contrary," replied Harley, "he was highly distressed about some family trouble, the nature of which he was about to confide to me when this sudden illness seized him."

He stared hard at Doctor McMurdoch, wondering how much he might hope to learn from him respecting the affairs of Sir Charles. It seemed almost impertinent at that hour to seek to pry into the dead man's private life.

To the quiet, book-lined apartment stole now and again little significant sounds which told of the tragedy in the household. Sometimes when a distant door was opened, it would be the sobs of a weeping woman, for the poor old housekeeper had been quite prostrated by the blow. Or ghostly movements would become audible from the room immediately over the library—the room to which the dead man had been carried: muffled footsteps, vague stirrings of furniture; each sound laden with its own peculiar portent, awakening the imagination which all too readily filled in the details of the scene above. Then, to spur Harley to action, came the thought that Sir Charles Abingdon had appealed to him for aid. Did his need terminate with his unexpected death or would the shadow under which he had died extend now Harley found himself staring across the library at the photograph of Phil Abingdon. It was of her that Sir Charles had been speaking when that mysterious seizure had tied his tongue. That strange, fatal illness, mused Harley, all the more strange in the case of a man supposedly in robust health—it almost seemed like the working of a malignant will. For the revelation, whatever its nature, had almost but not quite been made in Harley's office that evening. Something, some embarrassment or mental disability, had stopped Sir Charles from completing his statement. Tonight death had stopped him.

"Was he consulting you professionally, Mr. Harley?" asked the physician.

"He was," replied Harley, continuing to stare fascinatedly at the photograph on the mantelpiece. "I am informed," said he, abruptly, "that Miss Abingdon is out of town?"

Doctor McMurdoch nodded in his slow, gloomy fashion. "She is staying in Devonshire with poor Abingdon's sister," he answered. "I am wondering how we are going to break the news to her."

Perceiving that Doctor McMurdoch had clearly been intimate with the late Sir Charles, Harley determined to make use of this opportunity to endeavour to fathom the mystery of the late surgeon's fears. "You will not misunderstand me, Doctor McMurdoch," he said, "if I venture to ask you one or two rather personal questions respecting Miss Abingdon?"

Doctor McMurdoch lowered his shaggy brows and looked gloomily at the speaker. "Mr. Harley," he replied, "I know you by repute for a man of integrity. But before I answer your questions will you answer one of mine?"

"Certainly."

"Then my question is this: Does not your interest cease with the death of your client?"

"Doctor McMurdoch," said Harley, sternly, "you no doubt believe yourself to be acting as a friend of this bereaved family. You regard me, perhaps, as a Paul Pry prompted by idle curiosity. On the contrary, I find myself in a delicate and embarrassing situation. From Sir Charles's conversation I had gathered that he entertained certain fears on behalf of his daughter."

"Indeed," said Doctor McMurdoch.

"If these fears were well grounded, the danger is not removed, but merely increased by the death of Miss Abingdon's natural protector. I regret, sir, that I approached you for information, since you have misjudged my motive. But far from my interest having ceased, it has now as I see the matter become a sacred duty to learn what it was that Sir Charles apprehended. This duty, Doctor McMurdoch, I propose to fulfil with or without your assistance."

"Oh," said Doctor McMurdoch, gloomily, "I'm afraid I've offended you. But I meant well, Mr. Harley." A faint trace of human emotion showed itself in his deep voice. "Charley Abingdon and I were students together in Edinburgh," he explained. "I was mayhap a little strange."

His apology was so evidently sincere that Harley relented at once. "Please say no more, Doctor McMurdoch," he responded. "I fully appreciate your feelings in the matter. At such a time a stranger can only be an intruder, but"—he fixed his keen eyes upon the physician—"there is more underlying all this than you suspect or could readily believe. You will live to know that I have spoken the truth."

"I know it now," declared the Scotsman, solemnly. "Abingdon was always eccentric, but he didn't know the meaning of fear."

"Once that may have been true," replied Harley. "But a great fear was upon him when he came to me, Doctor McMurdoch, and if it is humanly possible I am going to discover its cause."

"Go ahead," said Doctor McMurdoch and, turning to the side table, he poured out two liberal portions of whiskey. "If there's anything I can do to help, count me at your service. You tell me he had fears about little Phil?"

"He had," answered Harley, "and it is maddening to think that he died before he could acquaint me with their nature. But I have hopes that you can help me in this. For instance"—again he fixed his gaze upon the gloomy face of the physician—"who is the distinguished Oriental gentleman with whom Sir Charles had recently become acquainted?"

Doctor McMurdoch's expression remained utterly blank, and he slowly shook his head. "I haven't an idea in the world," he declared. "A patient, perhaps?"

"Possibly," said Harley, conscious of some disappointment. "Yet from the way he spoke of him, I scarcely think that he was a patient. Surely Sir Charles, having resided so long in India, numbered several Orientals among his acquaintances if not among his friends?"

"None ever came to his home," replied Doctor McMurdoch. "He had all the Anglo-Indian's prejudice against men of colour." He rested his massive chin in his hand and stared down reflectively at the carpet.

"Then you have no suggestion to offer in regard to this person?"

"None. Did he tell you nothing further about him?"

"Unfortunately, nothing. In the next place, Doctor McMurdoch, are you aware of any difference of opinion which had arisen latterly between Sir Charles and his daughter?"

"Difference of opinion!" replied Doctor McMurdoch, raising his brows ironically. "There would always be difference of opinion between little Phil and any man who cared for her. But out-and-out quarrel—no!"

Again Harley found himself at a deadlock, and it was with scanty hope of success that he put his third question to the gloomy Scot. "Was Sir Charles a friend of Mr. Nicol Brinn?" he asked.

"Nicol Brinn?" echoed the physician. He looked perplexed. "You mean the American millionaire? I believe they were acquainted. Abingdon knew most of the extraordinary people in London, and if half one hears is true Nicol Brinn is as mad as a hatter. But they were not in any sense friends as far as I know." He was watching Harley curiously. "Why do you ask that question?"

"I will tell you in a moment," said Harley, rapidly, "but I have one more question to put to you first. Does the term Fire-Tongue convey anything to your mind?"

Doctor McMurdoch's eyebrows shot upward most amazingly. "I won't insult you by supposing that you have chosen such a time for joking," he said, dourly. "But if your third question surprised me, I must say that your fourth sounds simply daft."

"It must," agreed Harley, and his manner was almost fierce. "But when I tell you why I ask these two questions—and I only do so on the understanding that my words are to be treated in the strictest confidence—you may regard the matter in a new light. 'Nicol Brinn' and 'Fire-Tongue' were the last words which Sir Charles Abingdon uttered."

"What!" cried Doctor McMurdoch, displaying a sudden surprising energy. "What?"

"I solemnly assure you," declared Harley, "that such is the case. Benson, the butler, also overheard them."

Doctor McMurdoch relapsed once more into gloom, gazing at the whiskey in the glass which he held in his hand and slowly shaking his head. "Poor old Charley Abingdon," he murmured. "It's plain to me, Mr. Harley, that his mind was wandering. May not we find here an explanation, too, of this idea of his that some danger overhung Phil? You didn't chance to notice, I suppose, whether he had a temperature?"

"I did not," replied Harley, smiling slightly. But the smile quickly left his face, which became again grim and stern.

A short silence ensued, during which Doctor McMurdoch sat staring moodily down at the carpet and. Harley slowly paced up and down the room; then:

"In view of the fact," he said, suddenly, "that Sir Charles clearly apprehended an attempt upon his life, are you satisfied professionally that death was due to natural causes?"

"Perfectly satisfied," replied the physician, looking up with a start: "perfectly satisfied. It was unexpected, of course, but such cases are by no means unusual. He was formerly a keen athlete, remember. 'Tis often so. Surely you don't suspect foul play? I understood you to mean that his apprehensions were on behalf of Phil."

Paul Harley stood still, staring meditatively in the other's direction. "There is not a scrap of evidence to support such a theory," he admitted, "but if you knew of the existence of any poisonous agent which would produce effects simulating these familiar symptoms, I should be tempted to take certain steps."

"If you are talking about poisons," said the physician, a rather startled look appearing upon his face, "there are several I might mention, but the idea seems preposterous to me. Why should any one want to harm Charley Abingdon? When could poison have been administered and by whom?"

"When, indeed?" murmured Harley. "Yet I am not satisfied."

"You're not hinting at—suicide?"

"Emphatically no."

"What had he eaten?"

"Nothing but soup, except that he drank a portion of a glass of water. I am wondering if he took anything at Mr. Wilson's house." He stared hard at Doctor McMurdoch. "It may surprise you to learn that I have already taken steps to have the remains of the soup from Sir Charles's plate examined, as well as the water in the glass. I now propose to call upon Mr. Wilson in order that I may complete this line of enquiry."

"I sympathize with your suspicions, Mr. Harley," said the physician dourly, "but you are wasting your time." A touch of the old acidity crept back into his manner. "My certificate will be 'syncope due to unusual excitement,' and I shall stand by it."

"You are quite entitled to your own opinion," Harley conceded, "which if I were in your place would be my own. But what do you make of the fact that Sir Charles received a bogus telephone message some ten minutes before my arrival, as a result of which he visited Mr. Wilson's house?"

"But he's attending Wilson," protested the physician.

"Nevertheless, no one there had telephoned. It was a ruse. I don't assume for a moment that this ruse was purposeless."

Doctor McMurdoch was now staring hard at the speaker.

"You may also know," Harley continued, "that there was an attempted burglary here less than a week ago."

"I know that," admitted the other, "but it counts for little. There have been several burglaries in the neighbourhood of late."

Harley perceived that Doctor McMurdoch was one of those characters, not uncommon north of the Tweed, who, if slow in forming an opinion, once having done so cling to it as tightly as any barnacle.

"You may be right and I may be wrong," Harley admitted, "but while your professional business with Sir Charles unfortunately is ended, mine is only beginning. May I count upon you to advise me of Miss Abingdon's return? I particularly wish to see her, and I should prefer to meet her in the capacity of a friend rather than in that of a professional investigator."

"At the earliest moment that I can decently arrange a meeting," replied Doctor McMurdoch, "I will communicate with you, Mr. Harley. I am just cudgelling my brains at the moment to think how the news is to be broken to her. Poor little Phil! He was all she had."

"I wish I could help you," declared Harley with sincerity, "but in the circumstances any suggestion of mine would be mere impertinence." He held out his hand to the doctor.

"Good-night," said the latter, gripping it heartily. "If there is any mystery surrounding poor Abingdon's death, I believe you are the man to clear it up. But, frankly, it was his heart. I believe he had a touch of the sun once in India. Who knows? His idea that some danger threatened him or threatened Phil may have been merely—" He tapped his brow significantly.

"But in the whole of your knowledge of Sir Charles," cried Harley, exhibiting a certain irritation, "have you ever known him to suffer from delusions of that kind or any other?"

"Never," replied the physician, firmly. "But once a man has had the sun one cannot tell."

"Ah!" said Harley. "Good-night, Doctor McMurdoch."

When presently he left the house, carrying a brown leather bag which he had borrowed from the butler, he knew that rightly or wrongly his own opinion remained unchanged in spite of the stubborn opposition of the Scottish physician. The bogus message remained to be explained, and the assault in the square, as did the purpose of the burglar to whom gold and silver plate made no appeal. More important even than these points were the dead man's extraordinary words: "Fire-Tongue"—"Nicol Brinn." Finally and conclusively, he had detected the note of danger outside and inside the house; and now as he began to cross the square it touched him again intimately.

He looked up at the darkened sky. A black cloud was moving slowly overhead, high above the roof of the late Sir Charles Abingdon; and as he watched its stealthy approach it seemed to Paul Harley to be the symbol of that dread in which latterly Sir Charles's life had lain, beneath which he had died, and which now was stretching out, mysterious and menacing, over himself.

IV

INTRODUCING MR. NICOL BRINN

AT ABOUT NINE o'clock on the same evening, a man stood at a large window which over looked Piccadilly and the Green Park The room to which the window belonged was justly considered one of the notable sights of London and doubtless would have received suitable mention in the "Blue Guide" had the room been accessible to the general public. It was, on the contrary, accessible only to the personal friends of Mr. Nicol Brinn. As Mr. Nicol Brinn had a rarely critical taste in friendship, none but a fortunate few had seen the long room with its two large windows overlooking Piccadilly.

The man at the window was interested in a car which, approaching from the direction of the Circus, had slowed down immediately opposite and now was being turned, the chauffeur's apparent intention being to pull up at the door below. He had seen the face of the occupant and had recognized it even from that elevation. He was interested, and since only unusual things aroused any semblance of interest in the man who now stood at the window, one might have surmised that there was something unusual about the present visitor, or in his having decided to call at those chambers; and that such was indeed his purpose an upward glance which he cast in the direction of the balcony sufficiently proved.

The watcher, who had been standing in a dark recess formed by the presence of heavy velvet curtains draped before the window, now opened the curtains and stepped into the lighted room. He was a tall, lean man having straight, jet-black hair, a sallow complexion, and the features of a Sioux. A long black cigar protruded aggressively from the left corner of his mouth. His hands were locked behind him and his large and quite expressionless blue eyes stared straight across the room at the closed door with a dreamy and vacant regard. His dinner jacket fitted him so tightly that it might have been expected at any moment to split at the seams. As if to precipitate the catastrophe, he wore it buttoned.

There came a rap at the door.

"In!" said the tall man.

The door opened silently and a manservant appeared. He was spotlessly neat and wore his light hair cropped close to the skull. His fresh-coloured face was quite as expressionless as that of his master; his glance possessed no meaning. Crossing to the window, he extended a small salver upon which lay a visiting card.

"In!" repeated the tall man, looking down at the card.

His servant silently retired, and following a short interval rapped again upon the door, opened it, and standing just inside the room announced: "Mr. Paul Harley."

The door being quietly closed behind him, Paul Harley stood staring across the room at Nicol Brinn. At this moment the contrast between the types was one to have fascinated a psychologist. About Paul Harley, eagerly alert, there was something essentially British. Nicol Brinn, without being typical, was nevertheless distinctly a product of the United States. Yet, despite the stoic mask worn by Mr. Brinn, whose lack-lustre eyes were so unlike the bright gray eyes of his visitor, there existed, if not a physical, a certain spiritual affinity between the two; both were men of action.

Harley, after that one comprehensive glance, the photographic glance of a trained observer, stepped forward impulsively, hand outstretched. "Mr. Brinn," he said, "we have never met before, and it was good of you to wait in for me. I hope my telephone message has not interfered with your plans for the evening?"

Nicol Brinn, without change of pose, no line of the impassive face altering, shot out a large, muscular hand, seized that of Paul Harley in a tremendous grip, and almost instantly put his hand behind his back again. "Had no plans," he replied, in a high, monotonous voice. "I was bored stiff. Take the armchair."

Paul Harley sat down, but in the restless manner of one who has urgent business in hand and who is impatient of delay. Mr. Brinn stooped to a coffee table which stood upon the rug before the large open fireplace. "I am going to offer you a cocktail," he said.

"I shall accept your offer," returned Harley, smiling. "The 'N. B. cocktail' has a reputation which extends throughout the clubs of the world."

Nicol Brinn, exhibiting the swift adroitness of that human dodo, the New York bartender, mixed the drinks. Paul Harley watched him, meanwhile drumming his fingers restlessly upon the chair arm.

"Here's success," he said, "to my mission."

It was an odd toast, but Mr. Brinn merely nodded and drank in silence. Paul Harley set his glass down and glanced about the singular apartment of which he had often heard and which no man could ever tire of examining.

In this room the poles met, and the most remote civilizations of the world rubbed shoulders with modernity. Here, encased, were a family of snow-white ermine from Alaska and a pair of black Manchurian leopards. A flying lemur from the Pelews contemplated swooping upon the head of a huge tigress which glared with glassy eyes across the place at the snarling muzzle of a polar bear. Mycenaean vases and gold death masks stood upon the same shelf as Venetian goblets, and the mummy of an Egyptian priestess of the thirteenth dynasty occupied a sarcophagus upon the top of which rested a bas-relief found in one of the shrines of the Syrian fish goddess Derceto, at Ascalon.

Arrowheads of the Stone Age and medieval rapiers were ranged alongside some of the latest examples of the gunsmith's art. There were elephants' tusks and Mexican skulls, a stone jar of water from the well of Zem-Zem, and an ivory crucifix which had belonged to Torquemada. A mat of human hair from Borneo overlay a historical and unique rug woven in Ispahan and entirely composed of fragments of Holy Carpets from the Kaaba at Mecca.

"I take it," said Mr. Brinn, suddenly, "that you are up against a stiff proposition."

Paul Harley, accepting a cigarette from an ebony box (once the property of Henry VIII) which the speaker had pushed across the coffee table in his direction, stared up curiously into the sallow, aquiline face. "You are right. But how did you know?"

"You look that way. Also—you were followed. Somebody knows you've come here."

Harley leaned forward, resting one hand upon the table. "I know I was followed," he said, sternly. "I was followed because I have entered upon the biggest case of my career." He paused and smiled in a very grim fashion. "A suspicion begins to dawn upon my mind that if I fail it will also be my last case. You understand me?"

"I understand absolutely," replied Nicol Brinn. "These are dull days. It's meat and drink to me to smell big danger."

Paul Harley lighted a cigarette and watched the speaker closely the while. His expression, as he did so, was an odd one. Two courses were open to him, and he was mentally debating their respective advantages.

"I have come to you tonight, Mr. Brinn," he said finally, "to ask you a certain question. Unless the theory upon which I am working is entirely wrong, then, supposing that you are in a position to answer my question I am logically compelled to suppose, also, that you stand in peril of your life."

"Good," said Mr. Brinn. "I was getting sluggish." In three long strides he crossed the room and locked the door. "I don't doubt Hoskins's honesty," he explained, reading the inquiry in Harley's eyes, "but an A1 intelligence doesn't fold dress pants at thirty-nine."

Only one very intimate with the taciturn speaker could have perceived any evidence of interest in that imperturbable character. But Nicol Brinn took his cheroot between his fingers, quickly placed a cone of ash in a little silver tray (the work of Benvenuto Cellini), and replaced the cheroot not in the left but in the right corner of his mouth. He was excited.

"You are out after one of the big heads of the crook world," he said. "He knows it and he's trailing you. My luck's turned. How can I help?"

Harley stood up, facing Mr. Brinn. "He knows it, as you say," he replied, "and I hold my life in my hands. But from your answer to the question which I have come here tonight to ask you, I shall conclude whether or not your danger at the moment is greater than mine."

"Good," said Nicol Brinn.

In that unique room, at once library and museum, amid relics of a hundred ages, spoil of the chase, the excavator, and the scholar, these two faced each other; and despite the peaceful quiet of the apartment up to which as a soothing murmur stole the homely sounds of Piccadilly, each saw in the other's eyes recognition of a deadly peril. It was a queer, memorable moment.

"My question is simple but strange," said Paul Harley. "It is this: What do you know of 'Fire Tongue'?"

V

THE GATES OF HELL

IF PAUL HARLEY had counted upon the word "Fire-Tongue" to have a dramatic effect upon Nicol Brinn, he was not disappointed. It was a word which must have conveyed little or nothing to the multitude and which might have been pronounced without perceptible effect at any public meeting in the land. But Mr. Brinn, impassive though his expression remained, could not conceal the emotion which he experienced at the sound of it. His gaunt face seemed to grow more angular and his eyes to become even less lustrous.

"Fire-Tongue!" he said, tensely, following a short silence. "For God's sake, when did you hear that word?"

"I heard it," replied Harley, slowly, "tonight." He fixed his gaze intently upon the sallow face of the American. "It was spoken by Sir Charles Abingdon."

Closely as he watched Nicol Brinn while pronouncing this name he could not detect the slightest change of expression in the stoic features.

"Sir Charles Abingdon," echoed Brinn. "And in what way is it connected with your case?"

"In this way," answered Harley. "It was spoken by Sir Charles a few moments before he died."

Nicol Brinn's drooping lids flickered rapidly. "Before he died! Then Sir Charles Abingdon is dead! When did he die?"

"He died tonight and the last words that he uttered were 'Fire-Tongue'—" He paused, never for a moment removing that fixed gaze from the other's face.

"Go on," prompted Mr. Brinn.

"And 'Nicol Brinn.'"

Nicol Brinn stood still as a carven man. Indeed, only by an added rigidity in his pose did he reward Paul Harley's intense scrutiny. A silence charged with drama was finally broken by the American. "Mr. Harley," he said, "you told me that you were up against the big proposition of your career. You are right."

With that he sat down in an armchair and, resting his chin in his hand, gazed fixedly into the empty grate. His pose was that of a man who is suddenly called upon to review the course of his life and upon whose decision respecting the future that life may depend. Paul Harley watched him in silence.

"Give me the whole story," said Mr. Brinn, "right from the beginning." He looked up. "Do you know what you have done, Mr. Harley?"

Paul Harley shook his head. Swiftly, like the touch of an icy finger, that warning note of danger had reached him again.

"I'll tell you," continued Brinn. "You have opened the gates of hell!"

Not another word did he speak while Paul Harley, pacing slowly up and down before the hearth, gave him a plain account of the case, omitting all reference to his personal suspicions and to the measures which he had taken to confirm them.

He laid his cards upon the table deliberately. Whether Sir Charles Abingdon had uttered the name of Nicol Brinn as that of one whose aid should be sought or as a warning, he had yet to learn. And by this apparent frankness he hoped to achieve his object. That the celebrated American was in any way concerned in the menace which had overhung Sir Charles he was not prepared to believe. But he awaited with curiosity that explanation which Nicol Brinn must feel called upon to offer.

"You think he was murdered?" said Brinn in his high, toneless voice.

"I have formed no definite opinion. What is your own?"

"I may not look it," replied Brinn, "but at this present moment I am the most hopelessly puzzled and badly frightened man in London."

"Frightened?" asked Harley, curiously.

"I said frightened, I also said puzzled; and I am far too puzzled to be able to express any opinion respecting the death of Sir Charles Abingdon. When I tell you all I know of him you will wonder as much as I do, Mr. Harley, why my name should have been the last to pass his lips."

He half turned in the big chair to face his visitor, who now was standing before the fireplace staring down at him.

"One day last month," he resumed, "I got out of my car in a big hurry at the top of the Haymarket. A fool on a motorcycle passed between the car and the sidewalk just as I stepped down, and I knew nothing further until I woke up in a drug store close by, feeling very dazed and with my coat in tatters and my left arm numbed from the elbow. A man was standing watching me, and presently when I had pulled round he gave me his card.

"He was Sir Charles Abingdon, who had been passing at the time of the accident. That was how I met him, and as there was nothing seriously wrong with me I saw him no more professionally. But he dined with me a week later and I had lunch at his club about a fortnight ago."

He looked up at Harley. "On my solemn word of honour," he said, "that's all I know about Sir Charles Abingdon."

Paul Harley returned the other's fixed stare. "I don't doubt your assurance on the point, Mr. Brinn," he acknowledged. "I can well understand that you must be badly puzzled, but I would remind you of your statement that you were also frightened. Why?"

Nicol Brinn glanced rapidly about his own luxurious room in an oddly apprehensive manner. "I said that," he declared, "and I meant it."

"Then I can only suppose," resumed Harley, deliberately, "that the cause of your fear lies in the term, 'Fire-Tongue'?"

Brinn again rested his chin in his hand, staring fixedly into the grate.

"And possibly," went on the remorseless voice, "you can explain the significance of that term?"

Nicol Brinn remained silent—but with one foot he was slowly tapping the edge of the fender.

"Mr. Harley," he began, abruptly, "you have been perfectly frank with me and in return I wish to be as frank with you as I can be. I am face to face with a thing that has haunted me for seven years, and every step I take from now onward has to be considered carefully, for any step might be my last. And that's not the worst of the matter. I will risk one of those steps here and now. You ask me to explain the significance of Fire-Tongue . . ." (there was a perceptible pause before he pronounced the word, which Harley duly noticed.) "I am going to tell you that Sir Charles Abingdon, when I lunched with him at his club, asked me precisely the same thing."

"What! He asked you that so long as two weeks ago?"

"He did."

"And what reason did he give for his inquiry?"

Nicol Brinn began to tap the fender again with his foot. "Let me think," he replied. "I recognize that you must regard my reticence as peculiar, Mr. Harley, but if ever a man had reason to look before he leaped, I am that man."

Silence fell again, and Paul Harley, staring down at Nicol Brinn, realized that this indeed was the most hopelessly mystifying case which fate had ever thrown in his way. This millionaire scholar and traveller, whose figure was as familiar in remote cities of the world as it was familiar in New York, in Paris, and in London, could not conceivably be associated with any criminal organization. Yet his hesitancy was indeed difficult to explain, and because it seemed to Harley that the cloud which had stolen out across the house of Sir Charles Abingdon now hung threateningly over those very chambers, he merely waited and wondered.

"He referred to an experience which had befallen him in India," came Nicol Brinn's belated reply.

"In India? May I ask you to recount that experience?"

"Mr. Harley," replied Brinn, suddenly standing up, "I can't."

"You can't?"

"I have said so. But I'd give a lot more than you might believe to know that Abingdon had told you the story which he told me."

"You are not helping, Mr. Brinn," said Harley, sternly. "I believe and I think that you share my belief that Sir Charles Abingdon did not die from natural causes. You are repressing valuable evidence. Allow me to remind you that if anything should come to light necessitating a post-mortem examination of the body, you will be forced to divulge in a court of justice the facts which you refuse to divulge to me."

"I know it," said Brinn, shortly.

He shot out one long arm and grasped Harley's shoulder as in a vice. "I'm counted a wealthy man," he continued, "but I'd give every cent I possess to see 'paid' put to the bill of a certain person. Listen. You don't think I was in any way concerned in the death of Sir Charles Abingdon? It isn't thinkable. But you do think I'm in possession of facts which would help you find out who is. You're right."

"Good God!" cried Harley. "Yet you remain silent!"

"Not so loud—not so loud!" implored Brinn, repeating that odd, almost furtive glance around. "Mr. Harley—you know me. You've heard of me and now you've met me. You know my place in the world. Do you believe me when I say that from this moment onward I don't trust my own servants?"

"What! He asked you that so long as two weeks ago?"

"He did."

"And what reason did he give for his inquiry?"

Nicol Brinn began to tap the fender again with his foot. "Let me think," he replied. " I recognize that you must regard my reticence as peculiar, Mr. Harley, but if ever a man had reason to look before he leaped, I am that man."

Silence fell again, and Paul Harley, staring down at Nicol Brinn, realized that this indeed was the most hopelessly mystifying case which fate had ever thrown in his way. This millionaire scholar and traveller, whose figure was as familiar in remote cities of the world as it was familiar in New York, in Paris, and in London, could not conceivably be associated with any criminal organization. Yet his hesitancy was indeed difficult to explain, and because it seemed to Harley that the cloud which had stolen out across the house of Sir Charles Abingdon now hung threateningly over those very chambers, he merely waited and wondered.

"He referred to an experience which had befallen him in India," came Nicol Brinn's belated reply.

"In India? May I ask you to recount that experience?"

"Mr. Harley," replied Brinn, suddenly standing up, "I can't."

"You can't?"

"I have said so. But I'd give a lot more than you might believe to know that Abingdon had told you the story which he told me."

"You are not helping, Mr. Brinn," said Harley, sternly. "I believe and I think that you share my belief that Sir Charles Abingdon did not die from natural causes. You are repressing valuable evidence. Allow me to remind you that if anything should come to light necessitating a post-mortem examination of the body, you will be forced to divulge in a court of justice the facts which you refuse to divulge to me."

"I know it," said Brinn, shortly.

He shot out one long arm and grasped Harley's shoulder as in a vice. "I'm counted a wealthy man," he continued, "but I'd give every cent I possess to see 'paid' put to the bill of a certain person. Listen. You don't think I was in any way concerned in the death of Sir Charles Abingdon? It isn't thinkable. But you do think I'm in possession of facts which would help you find out who is. You're right."

"Good God!" cried Harley. "Yet you remain silent!"

"Not so loud—not so loud!" implored Brinn, repeating that odd, almost furtive glance around. "Mr. Harley—you know me. You've heard of me and now you've met me. You know my place in the world. Do you believe me when I say that from this moment onward I don't trust my own servants? Nor my own friends?" He removed his grip from Harley's shoulder. "Inanimate things look like enemies. That mummy over yonder may have ears!"

"I'm afraid I don't altogether understand you."

"See here!"

Nicol Brinn crossed to a bureau, unlocked it, and while Harley watched him curiously, sought among a number of press cuttings. Presently he found the cutting for which he was looking. "This was said," he explained, handing the slip to Harley, "at the Players' Club in New York, after a big dinner. It was said in confidence. But some disguised reporter had got in and it came out in print next morning. Read it."

Paul Harley accepted the cutting and read the following:

NICOL BRINN'S SECRET AMBITIONS: MILLIONAIRE SPORTSMAN WANTS TO SHOOT NIAGARA!

Mr. Nicol Brinn of Cincinnati, who is at present in New York, opened his heart to members of the Players' Club last night. Responding to a toast, the distinguished visitor said:

"I'd like to live through months of midnight frozen in among the polar ice; I'd like to cross Africa from east to west and get lost in the middle. I'd like to have a Montana sheriff's posse on my heels for horse stealing, and I've prayed to be wrecked on a desert island like Robinson Crusoe to see if I am man enough to live it out. I want to stand my trial for murder and defend my own case, and I want to be found by the eunuchs in the harem of the Shah. I want to dive for pearls and scale the Matterhorn. I want to know where the tunnel leads to—the tunnel down under the Great Pyramid of Gizeh—and I'd love to shoot Niagara Falls in a barrel."

"It sounds characteristic," murmured Harley, laying the slip on the coffee table.

"It's true!" declared Brinn. "I said it, and I meant it. I'm a glutton for danger, Mr. Harley, and I'm going to tell you why. Something happened to me seven years ago—"

"In India?"

"In India. Correct. Something happened to me, sir, which just took the sunshine out of life. At the time I didn't know all it meant. I've learned since. For seven years I have been flirting with death and hoping to fall!"

Harley stared at him uncomprehendingly. "More than ever I fail to understand."

"I can only ask you to be patient, Mr. Harley. Time is a wonderful doctor, and I don't say that in seven years the old wound hasn't healed a bit. But tonight you have, unknowingly, undone all that time had done. I'm a man that has been down into hell. I bought myself out. I thought I knew where the pit was located. I thought I was well away from it, Mr. Harley, and you have told me something tonight which makes me think that it isn't where I supposed at all, but hidden down here right under our feet in London. And we're both standing on the edge!"

That Nicol Brinn was deeply moved no student of humanity could have doubted. From beneath the stoic's cloak another than the daredevil millionaire whose crazy exploits were notorious had looked out. Persistently the note of danger came to Paul Harley. Those luxurious Piccadilly chambers were a focus upon which some malignant will was concentrated. He became conscious of anger. It was the anger of a just man who finds himself impotent—the rage of Prometheus bound.

"Mr. Brinn!" he cried, "I accept unreservedly all that you have told me. Its real significance I do not and cannot grasp. But my theory that Sir Charles Abingdon was done to death has become a conviction. That a like fate threatens yourself and possibly myself I begin to believe." He looked almost fiercely into the other's dull eyes. "My reputation east and west is that of a white man. Mr. Brinn—I ask you for your confidence."

Nicol Brinn dropped his chin into his hand and resumed that unseeing stare into the open grate. Paul Harley watched him intently.

"There isn't any one I would rather confide in," confessed the American. "We are linked by a common danger. But"—he looked up—"I must ask you again to be patient. Give me time to think—to make plans. For your own part—be cautious. You witnessed the death of Sir Charles Abingdon. You don't think and perhaps I don't think that it was natural; but whatever steps you may have taken to confirm your theories, I dare not hope that you will ever discover even a ghost of a clue. I simply warn you, Mr. Harley. You may go the same way. So may I. Others have travelled that road before poor Abingdon."

He suddenly stood up, all at once exhibiting to his watchful visitor that tremendous nervous energy which underlay his impassive manner. "Good God!" he said, in a cold, even voice. "To think that it is here in London. What does it mean?"

He ceased speaking abruptly, and stood with his elbow resting on a corner of the mantelpiece.

"You speak of it being here," prompted Harley. "Is it consistent with your mysterious difficulties to inform me to what you refer?"

Nicol Brinn glanced aside at him. "If I informed you of that," he answered, "you would know all you want to know. But neither you nor I would live to use the knowledge. Give me time. Let me think."

Silence fell in the big room, Nicol Brinn staring down vacantly into the empty fireplace, Paul Harley standing watching him in a state of almost stupefied mystification. Muffled to a soothing murmur the sounds of Piccadilly penetrated to that curtained chamber which held so many records of the troubled past and which seemed to be charged with shadowy portents of the future.

Something struck with a dull thud upon a windowpane—once—twice. There followed a faint, sibilant sound.

Paul Harley started and the stoical Nicol Brinn turned rapidly and glanced across the room.

"What was that?" asked Harley.

"I expect—it was an owl," answered Brinn. "We sometimes get them over from the Green Park."

His high voice sounded unemotional as ever. But it seemed to Paul Harley that his face, dimly illuminated by the upcast light from the lamp upon the coffee table, had paled, had become gaunt.

VI

PHIL ABINGDON ARRIVES

ON THE FOLLOWING afternoon Paul Harley was restlessly pacing his private office when Innes came in with a letter which had been delivered by hand. Harley took it eagerly and tore open the envelope. A look of expectancy faded from his eager face almost in the moment that it appeared there. "No luck, Innes," he said, gloomily. "Merton reports that there is no trace of any dangerous foreign body in the liquids analyzed."

He dropped the analyst's report into a wastebasket and resumed his restless promenade. Innes, who could see that his principal wanted to talk, waited. For it was Paul Harley's custom, when the clue to a labyrinth evaded him, to outline his difficulties to his confidential secretary, and by the mere exercise of verbal construction Harley would often detect the weak spot in his reasoning. This stage come to, he would dictate a carefully worded statement of the case to date and thus familiarize himself with its complexities.

"You see, Innes," he began, suddenly, "Sir Charles had taken no refreshment of any kind at Mr. Wilson's house nor before leaving his own. Neither had he smoked. No one had approached him. Therefore, if he was poisoned, he was poisoned at his own table. Since he was never out of my observation from the moment of entering the library up to that of his death, we are reduced to the only two possible mediums—the soup or the water. He had touched nothing else."

"No wine?"

"Wine was on the table but none had been poured out. Let us see what evidence, capable of being put into writing, exists to support my theory that Sir Charles was poisoned. In the first place, he clearly went in fear of some such death. It was because of this that he consulted me. What was the origin of his fear? Something associated with the term Fire-Tongue. So much is clear from Sir Charles's dying words, and his questioning Nicol Brinn on the point some weeks earlier.

"He was afraid, then, of something or someone linked in his mind with the word Fire-Tongue. What do we know about Fire-Tongue? One thing only: that it had to do with some episode which took place in India. This item we owe to Nicol Brinn.

"Very well. Sir Charles believed himself to be in danger from something or person unknown, associated with India and with the term Fire-Tongue. What else? His house was entered during the night under circumstances suggesting that burglary was not the object of the entrance. And next? He was assaulted, with murderous intent. Thirdly, he believed himself to be subjected to constant surveillance. Was this a delusion? It was not. After failing several times I myself detected someone dogging my movements last night at the moment I entered Nicol Brinn's chambers. Nicol Brinn also saw this person.

"In short, Sir Charles was, beyond doubt, at the time of his death, receiving close attention from some mysterious person or persons the object of which he believed to be his death. Have I gone beyond established facts, Innes, thus far?"

"No, Mr. Harley. So far you are on solid ground."

"Good. Leaving out of the question those points which we hope to clear up when the evidence of Miss Abingdon becomes available—how did Sir Charles learn that Nicol Brinn knew the meaning of Fire-Tongue?"

"He may have heard something to that effect in India."

"If this were so he would scarcely have awaited a chance encounter to prosecute his inquiries, since Nicol Brinn is a well-known figure in London and Sir Charles had been home for several years."

"Mr. Brinn may have said something after the accident and before he was in full possession of his senses which gave Sir Charles a clue."

"He did not, Innes. I called at the druggist's establishment this morning. They recalled the incident, of course. Mr. Brinn never uttered a word until, opening his eyes, he said: 'Hello! Am I much damaged?'"

Innes smiled discreetly. "A remarkable character, Mr. Harley," he said. "Your biggest difficulty at the moment is to fit Mr. Nicol Brinn into the scheme."

"He won't fit at all, Innes! We come to the final and conclusive item of evidence substantiating my theory of Sir Charles's murder: Nicol Brinn believes he was murdered. Nicol Brinn has known others, in his own words, 'to go the same way.' Yet Nicol Brinn, a millionaire, a scholar, a sportsman, and a gentleman, refuses to open his mouth."

"He is afraid of something."

"He is afraid of Fire-Tongue—whatever Fire-Tongue may be! I never saw a man of proved courage more afraid in my life. He prefers to court arrest for complicity in a murder rather than tell what he knows!"

"It's unbelievable."

"It would be, Innes, if Nicol Brinn's fears were personal."

Paul Harley checked his steps in front of the watchful secretary and gazed keenly into his eyes.

"Death has no terrors for Nicol Brinn," he said slowly. "All his life he has toyed with danger. He admitted to me that during the past seven years he had courted death. Isn't it plain enough, Innes? If ever a man possessed all that the world had to offer, Nicol Brinn is that man. In such a case and in such circumstances what do we look for?"

Innes shook his head.

"We look for the woman!" snapped Paul Harley.

There came a rap at the door and Miss Smith, the typist, entered. "Miss Phil Abingdon and Doctor McMurdoch," she said.

"Good heavens!" muttered Harley. "So soon? Why, she can only just—" He checked himself. "Show them in, Miss Smith," he directed.

As the typist went out, followed by Innes, Paul Harley found himself thinking of the photograph in Sir Charles Abingdon's library and waiting with an almost feverish expectancy for the appearance of the original.

Almost immediately Phil Abingdon came in, accompanied by the sepulchral Doctor McMurdoch. And Harley found himself wondering whether her eyes were really violet-coloured or whether intense emotion heroically repressed had temporarily lent them that appearance.

Surprise was the predominant quality of his first impression. Sir Charles Abingdon's daughter was so exceedingly vital—petite and slender, yet instinct with force. The seeming repose of the photograph was misleading. That her glance could be naive he realized—as it could also be gay—and now her eyes were sad with a sadness so deep as to dispel the impression of lightness created by her dainty form, her alluring, mobile lips, and the fascinating, wavy, red-brown hair.

She did not wear mourning. He recalled that there had been no time to procure it. She was exquisitely and fashionably dressed, and even the pallor of grief could not rob her cheeks of the bloom born of Devon sunshine. He had expected her to be pretty. He was surprised to find her lovely.

Doctor McMurdoch stood silent in the doorway, saying nothing by way of introduction. But nothing was necessary. Phil Abingdon came forward quite naturally—and quite naturally Paul Harley discovered her little gloved hand to lie clasped between both his own. It was more like a reunion than a first meeting and was so laden with perfect understanding that, even yet, speech seemed scarcely worth while.

Thinking over that moment, in later days, Paul Harley remembered that he had been prompted by some small inner voice to say: "So you have come back?" It was recognition. Of the hundreds of men and women who came into his life for a while, and ere long went out of it again, he knew, by virtue of that sixth sense of his, that Phil Abingdon had come to stay—whether for joy or sorrow he could not divine.

It was really quite brief—that interval of silence—although perhaps long enough to bridge the ages.

"How brave of you, Miss Abingdon!" said Harley. "How wonderfully brave of you!"

"She's an Abingdon," came the deep tones of Doctor McMurdoch. "She arrived only two hours ago and here she is."

"There can be no rest for me, Doctor," said the girl, and strove valiantly to control her voice, "until this dreadful doubt is removed. Mr. Harley"—she turned to him appealingly—"please don't study my feelings in the least; I can bear anything—now; just tell me what happened.

Oh! I had to come. I felt that I had to come."

As Paul Harley placed an armchair for his visitor, his glance met that of Doctor McMurdoch, and in the gloomy eyes he read admiration of this girl who could thus conquer the inherent weakness of her sex and at such an hour and after a dreadful ordeal set her hand to the task which fate had laid upon her.

Doctor McMurdoch sat down on a chair beside the door, setting his silk hat upon the floor and clasping his massive chin with his hand.

"I will endeavour to do as you wish, Miss Abingdon." said Harley, glancing anxiously at the physician.

But Doctor McMurdoch returned only a dull stare. It was evident that this man of stone was as clay in the hands of Phil Abingdon. He deprecated the strain which she was imposing upon her nervous system, already overwrought to the danger point, but he was helpless for all his dour obstinacy. Harley, looking down at the girl's profile, read a new meaning into the firm line of her chin. He was conscious of an insane desire to put his arms around this new acquaintance who seemed in some indefinable yet definite way to belong to him and to whisper the tragic story he had to tell, comforting her the while.

He began to relate what had taken place at the first interview, when Sir Charles had told him of the menace which he had believed to hang over his life. He spoke slowly, deliberately, choosing his words with a view to sparing Phil Abingdon's feelings as far as possible.

She made no comment throughout, but her fingers alternately tightened and relaxed their hold upon the arms of the chair in which she was seated. Once, at some reference to words spoken by her father, her sensitive lips began to quiver and Harley, watching her, paused. She held the chair arms more tightly. "Please go on, Mr. Harley," she said.

The words were spoken in a very low voice, but the speaker looked up bravely, and Harley, reassured, proceeded uninterruptedly to the end of the story. Then:

"At some future time, Miss Abingdon," he concluded, "I hope you will allow me to call upon you. There is so much to be discussed—"

Again Phil Abingdon looked up into his face. "I have forced myself to come to see you today," she said, "because I realize there is no service I can do poor dad so important as finding out—"

"I understand," Harley interrupted, gently. "But—"

"No, no." Phil Abingdon shook her head rebelliously. "Please ask me what you want to know. I came for that."

He met the glance of violet eyes, and understood something of Doctor McMurdoch's helplessness. He found his thoughts again wandering into strange, wild byways and was only recalled to the realities by the dry, gloomy voice of the physician. "Go on, Mr. Harley," said Doctor McMurdoch. "She has grand courage."

VII

CONFESSIONS

PAUL HARLEY CROSSED the room and stood in front of the tall Burmese cabinet. He experienced the utmost difficulty in adopting a judicial attitude toward his beautiful visitor. Proximity increased his mental confusion. Therefore he stood on the opposite side of the office ere beginning to question her.

"In the first place, Miss Abingdon," he said, speaking very deliberately, "do you attach any particular significance to the term 'Fire-Tongue'?"

Phil Abingdon glanced rapidly at Doctor McMurdoch. "None at all, Mr. Harley," she replied. "The doctor has already told me of—"

"You know why I ask?" She inclined her head.

"And Mr. Nicol Brinn? Have you met this gentleman?"

"Never. I know that Dad had met him and was very much interested in him."

"In what way?"

"I have no idea. He told me that he thought Mr. Brinn one of the most singular characters he had ever known. But beyond describing his rooms in Piccadilly, which had impressed him as extraordinary, he said very little about Mr. Brinn. He sounded interesting and"—she hesitated and her eyes filled with tears—"I asked Dad to invite him home." Again she paused. This retrospection, by making the dead seem to live again, added to the horror of her sudden bereavement, and Harley would most gladly have spared her more. "Dad seemed strangely disinclined to do so," she added.

At that the keen investigator came to life within Harley. "Your father did not appear anxious to bring Mr. Brinn to his home?" he asked.

"Not at all anxious. This was all the more strange because Dad invited Mr. Brinn to his club."

"He gave no reason for his refusal?"

"Oh, there was no refusal, Mr. Harley. He merely evaded the matter. I never knew why."

"H'm," muttered Harley. "And now, Miss Abingdon, can you enlighten me respecting the identity of the Oriental gentleman with whom he had latterly become acquainted?"

Phil Abingdon glanced rapidly at Doctor McMurdoch and then lowered her head. She did not answer at once. "I know to whom you refer, Mr. Harley," she said, finally. "But it was I who had made this gentleman's acquaintance. My father did not know him."

"Then I wonder why he mentioned him?" murmured Harley.

"That I cannot imagine. I have been wondering ever since Doctor McMurdoch told me."

"You recognize the person to whom Sir Charles referred?"

"Yes. He could only have meant Ormuz Khan."

"Ormuz Khan—" echoed Harley. "Where have I heard that name?"

"He visits England periodically, I believe. In fact, he has a house somewhere near London. I met him at Lady Vail's."

"Lady Vail's? His excellency moves, then, in diplomatic circles? Odd that I cannot place him."

"I have a vague idea, Mr. Harley, that he is a financier. I seem to have heard that he had something to do with the Imperial Bank of Iran." She glanced naively at Harley. "Is there such a bank?" she asked.

"There is," he replied. "Am I to understand that Ormuz Khan is a Persian?"

"I believe he is a Persian," said Phil Abingdon, rather confusedly. "To be quite frank, I know very little about him."

Paul Harley gazed steadily at the speaker for a moment. "Can you think of any reason why Sir Charles should have worried about this gentleman?" he asked.

The girl lowered her head again. "He paid me a lot of attention," she finally confessed.

"This meeting at Lady Vail's, then, was the first of many?"

"Oh, no—not of many! I saw him two or three times. But he began to send me most extravagant presents. I suppose it was his Oriental way of paying a compliment, but Dad objected."

"Of course he would. He knew his Orient and his Oriental. I assume, Miss Abingdon, that you were in England during the years that your father lived in the East?"

"Yes. I was at school. I have never been in the East."

Paul Harley hesitated. He found himself upon dangerously delicate ground and was temporarily at a loss as to how to proceed. Unexpected aid came from the taciturn Doctor McMurdoch.

"He never breathed a word of this to me, Phil," he said, gloomily. "The impudence of the man! Small wonder Abingdon objected."

Phil Abingdon tilted her chin forward rebelliously.

"Ormuz Khan was merely unfamiliar with English customs," she retorted. "There was nothing otherwise in his behaviour to which any one could have taken exception."

"What's that!" demanded the physician. "If a man of colour paid his heathen attentions to my daughter—"

"But you have no daughter, Doctor."

"No. But if I had—"

"If you had," echoed Phil Abingdon, and was about to carry on this wordy warfare which, Harley divined, was of old standing between the two, when sudden realization of the purpose of the visit came to her. She paused, and he saw her biting her lips desperately. Almost at random he began to speak again.

"So far as you are aware, then, Miss Abingdon, Sir Charles never met Ormuz Khan?"

"He never even saw him, Mr. Harley, that I know of."

"It is most extraordinary that he should have given me the impression that this man—for I can only suppose that he referred to Ormuz Khan—was in some way associated with his fears."

"I must remind you, Mr. Harley," Doctor McMurdoch interrupted, "that poor Abingdon was a free talker. His pride, I take it, which was strong, had kept him silent on this matter with me, but he welcomed an opportunity of easing his mind to one discreet and outside the family circle. His words to you may have had no bearing upon the thing he wished to consult you about."

"H'm," mused Harley. "That's possible. But such was not my impression."

He turned again to Phil Abingdon. "This Ormuz Khan, I understood you to say, actually resides in or near London?"

"He is at present living at the Savoy, I believe. He also has a house somewhere outside London."

There were a hundred other questions Paul Harley was anxious to ask: some that were professional but more that were personal. He found himself resenting the intrusion of this wealthy Oriental into the life of the girl who sat there before him. And because he could read a kindred resentment in the gloomy eye of Doctor McMurdoch, he was drawn spiritually closer to that dour character.

By virtue of his training he was a keen psychologist, and he perceived clearly enough that Phil Abingdon was one of those women in whom a certain latent perversity is fanned to life by opposition. Whether she was really attracted by Ormuz Khan or whether she suffered his attentions merely because she knew them to be distasteful to others, he could not yet decide.

Anger threatened him—as it had threatened him when he had realized that Nicol Brinn meant to remain silent. He combated it, for it had no place in the judicial mind of the investigator. But he recognized its presence with dismay. Where Phil Abingdon was concerned he could not trust himself. In her glance, too, and in the manner of her answers to questions concerning the Oriental, there was a provoking femininity—a deliberate and baffling intrusion of the eternal Eve.

He stared questioningly across at Doctor McMurdoch and perceived a sudden look of anxiety in the physician's face. Quick as the thought which the look inspired, he turned to Phil Abingdon.

She was sitting quite motionless in the big armchair, and her face had grown very pale. Even as he sprang forward he saw her head droop.

"She has fainted," said Doctor McMurdoch. "I'm not surprised."

"Nor I," replied Harley. "She should not have come."

He opened the door communicating with his private apartments and ran out. But, quick as he was, Phil Abingdon had recovered before he returned with the water for which he had gone. Her reassuring smile was somewhat wan. "How perfectly silly of me!" she said. "I shall begin to despise myself."

Presently he went down to the street with his visitors.

"There must be so much more you want to know, Mr. Harley," said Phil Abingdon. "Will you come and see me?"

He promised to do so. His sentiments were so strangely complex that he experienced a desire for solitude in order that he might strive to understand them. As he stood at the door watching the car move toward the Strand he knew that today he could not count upon his intuitive powers to warn him of sudden danger. But he keenly examined the faces of passers-by and stared at the occupants of those cabs and cars which were proceeding in the same direction as the late Sir Charles Abingdon's limousine.

No discovery rewarded him, however, and he returned upstairs to his office deep in thought. "I am in to nobody," he said as he passed the desk at which Innes was at work.

"Very good, Mr. Harley."

Paul Harley walked through to the private office and, seating himself at the big, orderly table, reached over to a cupboard beside him and took out a tin of smoking mixture. He began very slowly to load his pipe, gazing abstractedly across the room at the tall Burmese cabinet.

He realized that, excepting the extraordinary behaviour and the veiled but significant statements of Nicol Brinn, his theory that Sir Charles Abingdon had not died from natural causes rested upon data of the most flimsy description. From Phil Abingdon he had learned nothing whatever. Her evidence merely tended to confuse the case more hopelessly.

It was sheer nonsense to suppose that Ormuz Khan, who was evidently interested in the girl, could be in any way concerned in the death of her father. Nevertheless, as an ordinary matter of routine, Paul Harley, having lighted his pipe, made a note on a little block:

Cover activities of Ormuz Khan.

He smoked reflectively for a while and then added another note:

Watch Nicol Brinn.

For ten minutes or more he sat smoking and thinking, his unseeing gaze set upon the gleaming lacquer of the cabinet; and presently, as he smoked, he became aware of an abrupt and momentary chill.

His sixth sense was awake again. Taking up a pencil, he added a third note:

Watch yourself. You are in danger.

VIII

A WREATH OF HYACINTHS

DEEP IN REFLECTION and oblivious of the busy London life around him, Paul Harley walked slowly along the Strand. Outwardly he was still the keen-eyed investigator who could pry more deeply into a mystery than any other in England; but today his mood was introspective. He was in a brown study.

The one figure which had power to recall him to the actual world suddenly intruded itself upon his field of vision. From dreams which he recognized in the moment of awakening to have been of Phil Abingdon, he was suddenly aroused to the fact that Phil Abingdon herself was present. Perhaps, half subconsciously, he had been looking for her.

Veiled and dressed in black, he saw her slim figure moving through the throng. He conceived the idea that there was something furtive in her movements. She seemed to be hurrying along as if desirous of avoiding recognition. Every now and again she glanced back, evidently in search of a cab, and a dormant suspicion which had lain in Harley's mind now became animate. Phil Abingdon was coming from the direction of the Savoy Hotel. Was it possible that she had been to visit Ormuz Khan?

Harley crossed the Strand and paused just in front of the hurrying, black-clad figure. "Miss Abingdon," he said, "a sort of instinct told me that I should meet you today."

She stopped suddenly, and through the black veil which she wore he saw her eyes grow larger—or such was the effect as she opened them widely. Perhaps he misread their message. To him Phil Abingdon's expression was that of detected guilt. More than ever he was convinced of the truth of his suspicions. "Perhaps you were looking for a cab?" he suggested.

Overcoming her surprise, or whatever emotion had claimed her at the moment of this unexpected meeting, Phil Abingdon took Harley's outstretched hand and held it for a moment before replying. "I had almost despaired of finding one," she said, "and I am late already."

"The porter at the Savoy would get you one."

"I have tried there and got tired of waiting," she answered quite simply.

For a moment Harley's suspicions were almost dispelled, and, observing an empty cab approaching, he signalled to the man to pull up.

"Where do you want to go to?" he inquired, opening the door.

"I am due at Doctor McMurdoch's," she replied, stepping in.

Paul Harley hesitated, glancing from the speaker to the driver.

"I wonder if you have time to come with me," said Phil Abingdon. "I know the doctor wants to see you."

"I will come with pleasure," replied Harley, a statement which was no more than true.

Accordingly he gave the necessary directions to the taxi man and seated himself beside the girl in the cab.

"I am awfully glad of an opportunity of a chat with you, Mr. Harley," said Phil Abingdon. "The last few days have seemed like one long nightmare to me." She sighed pathetically. "Surely Doctor McMurdoch is right, and all the horrible doubts which troubled us were idle ones, after all?"

She turned to Harley, looking almost eagerly into his face. "Poor daddy hadn't an enemy in the world, I am sure," she said. "His extraordinary words to you no doubt have some simple explanation. Oh, it would be such a relief to know that his end was a natural one. At least it would dull the misery of it all a little bit."

The appeal in her eyes was of a kind which Harley found much difficulty in resisting. It would have been happiness to offer consolation to this sorrowing girl. But, although he could not honestly assure her that he had abandoned his theories, he realized that the horror of her suspicions was having a dreadful effect upon Phil Abingdon's mind.

"You may quite possibly be right," he said, gently. "In any event, I hope you will think as little as possible about the morbid side of this unhappy business."

"I try to," she assured him, earnestly, "but you can imagine how hard the task is. I know that you must have some good reason for your idea; something, I mean, other than the mere words which have puzzled us all so much. Won't you tell me?"

Now, Paul Harley had determined, since the girl was unacquainted with Nicol Brinn, to conceal from her all that he had learned from that extraordinary man. In this determination he had been actuated, too, by the promptings of the note of danger which, once seemingly attuned to the movements of Sir Charles Abingdon, had, after the surgeon's death, apparently become centred upon himself and upon Nicol Brinn. He dreaded the thought that the cloud might stretch out over the life of this girl who sat beside him and whom he felt so urgently called upon to protect from such a menace.

The cloud? What was this cloud, whence did it emanate, and by whom had it been called into being? He looked into the violet eyes, and as a while before he had moved alone through the wilderness of London now he seemed to be alone with Phil Abingdon on the border of a spirit world which had no existence for the multitudes around. Psychically, he was very close to her at that moment; and when he replied he replied evasively: "I have absolutely no scrap of evidence, Miss Abingdon, pointing to foul play. The circumstances were peculiar, of course, but I have every confidence in Doctor McMurdoch's efficiency. Since he is satisfied, it would be mere impertinence on my part to question his verdict."

Phil Abingdon repeated the weary sigh and turned her head aside, glancing down to where with one small shoe she was restlessly tapping the floor of the cab. They were both silent for some moments.

"Don't you trust me?" she asked, suddenly. "Or don't you think I am clever enough to share your confidence?"

As she spoke she looked at him challengingly, and he felt all the force of personality which underlay her outward lightness of manner.

"I both trust you and respect your intelligence," he answered, quietly. "If I withhold anything from you, I am prompted by a very different motive from the one you suggest."

"Then you are keeping something from me," she said, softly. "I knew you were."

"Miss Abingdon," replied Harley, "when the worst trials of this affair are over, I want to have a long talk with you. Until then, won't you believe that I am acting for the best?"

But Phil Abingdon's glance was unrelenting.

"In your opinion it may be so, but you won't do me the honour of consulting mine."

Harley had half anticipated this attitude, but had hoped that she would not adopt it. She possessed in a high degree the feminine art of provoking a quarrel. But he found much consolation in the fact that she had thus shifted the discussion from the abstract to the personal. He smiled slightly, and Phil Abingdon's expression relaxed in response and she lowered her eyes quickly. "Why do you persistently treat me like a child?" she said.

"I don't know," replied Harley, delighted but bewildered by her sudden change of mood. "Perhaps because I want to."

She did not answer him, but stared abstractedly out of the cab window; and Harley did not break this silence, much as he would have liked to do so. He was mentally reviewing his labours of the preceding day when, in the character of a Colonial visitor with much time on his hands, he had haunted the Savoy for hours in the hope of obtaining a glimpse of Ormuz Khan. His vigil had been fruitless, and on returning by a roundabout route to his office he had bitterly charged himself with wasting valuable time upon a side issue. Yet when, later, he had sat in his study endeavouring to arrange his ideas in order, he had discovered many points in his own defence.

If his ineffective surveillance of Ormuz Khan had been dictated by interest in Phil Abingdon rather than by strictly professional motives, it was, nevertheless, an ordinary part of the conduct of such a case. But while he had personally undertaken the matter of his excellency he had left the work of studying the activities of Nicol Brinn to an assistant. He could not succeed in convincing himself that, on the evidence available, the movements of the Oriental gentleman were more important than those of the American.

"Here we are," said Phil Abingdon.

She alighted, and Harley dismissed the cabman and followed the girl into Doctor McMurdoch's house. Here he made the acquaintance of Mrs. McMurdoch, who, as experience had taught him to anticipate, was as plump and merry and vivacious as her husband was lean, gloomy, and taciturn. But she was a perfect well of sympathy, as her treatment of the bereaved girl showed. She took her in her arms and hugged her in a way that was good to see.

"We were waiting for you, dear," she said when the formality of presenting Harley was over. "Are you quite sure that you want to go?"

Phil Abingdon nodded pathetically. She had raised her veil, and Harley could see that her eyes were full of tears. "I should like to see the flowers," she answered.

She was staying at the McMurdoch's house, and as the object at present in view was that of a visit to her old home, from which the funeral of Sir Charles Abingdon was to take place on the morrow, Harley became suddenly conscious of the fact that his presence was inopportune.

"I believe you want to see me, Doctor McMurdoch," he said, turning to the dour physician. "Shall I await your return or do you expect to be detained?"

But Phil Abingdon had her own views on the matter. She stepped up beside him and linked her arm in his.

"Please come with me, Mr. Harley," she pleaded. "I want you to."

As a result he found himself a few minutes later entering the hall of the late Sir Charles's house. The gloved hand resting on his arm trembled, but when he looked down solicitously into Phil Abingdon's face she smiled bravely, and momentarily her clasp tightened as if to reassure him.

It seemed quite natural that she should derive comfort from the presence of this comparative stranger; and neither of the two, as they stood there looking at the tributes to the memory of the late Sir Charles—which overflowed from a neighbouring room into the lobby and were even piled upon the library table—were conscious of any strangeness in the situation.

The first thing that had struck Harley on entering the house had been an overpowering perfume of hyacinths. Now he saw whence it arose; for, conspicuous amid the wreaths and crosses, was an enormous device formed of hyacinths. Its proportions dwarfed those of all the others.

Mrs. Howett, the housekeeper, a sad-eyed little figure, appeared now from behind the bank of flowers. Her grief could not rob her of that Old World manner which was hers, and she saluted the visitors with a bow which promised to develop into a curtsey. Noting the direction of Phil Abingdon's glance, which was set upon a card attached to the wreath of hyacinths: "It was the first to arrive, Miss Phil," she said. "Isn't it beautiful?"

"It's wonderful," said the girl, moving forward and drawing Harley along with her. She glanced from the card up to his face, which was set in a rather grim expression.

"Ormuz Khan has been so good," she said. "He sent his secretary to see if he could be of any assistance yesterday, but I certainly had not expected this."

Her eyes filled with tears again, and, because he thought they were tears of gratitude, Harley clenched his hand tightly so that the muscles of his forearm became taut to Phil Abingdon's touch. She looked up at him, smiling pathetically: "Don't you think it was awfully kind of him?" she asked.

"Very," replied Harley.

A dry and sepulchral cough of approval came from Doctor McMurdoch; and Harley divined with joy that when the ordeal of the next day was over Phil Abingdon would have to face cross-examination by the conscientious Scotsman respecting this stranger whose attentions, if Orientally extravagant, were instinct with such generous sympathy.

For some reason the heavy perfume of the hyacinths affected him unpleasantly. All his old doubts and suspicions found a new life, so that his share in the conversation which presently arose became confined to a few laconic answers to direct questions.

He was angry, and his anger was more than half directed against himself, because he knew that he had no shadow of right to question this girl about her friendships or even to advise her. He determined, however, even at the cost of incurring a rebuke, to urge Doctor McMurdoch to employ all the influence he possessed to terminate an acquaintanceship which could not be otherwise than undesirable, if it was not actually dangerous.

When, presently, the party returned to the neighbouring house of the physician, however, Harley's plans in this respect were destroyed by the action of Doctor McMurdoch, in whose composition tact was not a predominant factor. Almost before they were seated in the doctor's drawing room he voiced his disapproval. "Phil," he said, ignoring a silent appeal from his wife, "this is, mayhap, no time to speak of the matter, but I'm not glad to see the hyacinths."

Phil Abingdon's chin quivered rebelliously, and, to Harley's dismay, it was upon him that she fixed her gaze in replying. "Perhaps you also disapprove of his excellency's kindness?" she said, indignantly.

Harley found himself temporarily at a loss for words. She was perfectly well aware that he disapproved, and now was taking a cruel pleasure in reminding him of the fact that he was not entitled to do so. Had he been capable of that calm analysis to which ordinarily he submitted all psychological problems, he must have found matter for rejoicing in this desire of the girl's to hurt him. "I am afraid, Miss Abingdon," he replied, quietly, "that the matter is not one in which I am entitled to express my opinion."

She continued to look at him challengingly, but:

"Quite right, Mr. Harley," said Doctor McMurdoch, "but if you were, your opinion would be the same as mine."

Mrs. McMurdoch's glance became positively beseeching, but the physician ignored it. "As your father's oldest friend," he continued, "I feel called upon to remark that it isn't usual for strangers to thrust their attentions upon a bereaved family."

"Oh," said Phil Abingdon with animation, "do I understand that this is also your opinion, Mr. Harley?"

"As a man of the world," declared Doctor McMurdoch, gloomily, "it cannot fail to be."

Tardily enough he now succumbed to the silent entreaties of his wife. "I will speak of this later," he concluded. "Mayhap I should not have spoken now."

Tears began to trickle down Phil Abingdon's cheeks.

"Oh, my dear, my dear!" cried little Mrs. McMurdoch, running to her side.

But the girl sprang up, escaping from the encircling arm of the motherly old lady. She shook her head disdainfully, as if to banish tears and weakness, and glanced rapidly around from face to face. "I think you are all perfectly cruel and horrible," she said in a choking voice, turned, and ran out.

A distant door banged.

"H'm," muttered Doctor McMurdoch, "I've put my foot in it."

His wife looked at him in speechless indignation and then followed Phil Abingdon from the room.

IX

TWO REPORTS

ON RETURNING TO his office Paul Harley found awaiting him the report of the man to whom he had entrusted the study of the movements of Nicol Brinn. His mood was a disturbed one, and he had observed none of his customary precautions in coming from Doctor McMurdoch's house. He wondered if the surveillance which he had once detected had ceased. Perhaps the chambers of Nicol Brinn were the true danger zone upon which these subtle but powerful forces now were focused. On the other hand, he was quite well aware that his movements might have been watched almost uninterruptedly since the hour that Sir Charles Abingdon had visited his office.

During the previous day, in his attempt to learn the identity of Ormuz Khan, he had covered his tracks with his customary care. He had sufficient faith in his knowledge of disguise, which was extensive, to believe that those mysterious persons who were interested in his movements remained unaware of the fact that the simple-minded visitor from Vancouver who had spent several hours in and about the Savoy, and Paul Harley of Chancery Lane, were one and the same.

His brain was far too alertly engaged with troubled thoughts of Phil Abingdon to be susceptible to the influence of those delicate etheric waves which he had come to recognize as the note of danger. Practically there had been no development whatever in the investigation, and he was almost tempted to believe that the whole thing was a mirage, when the sight of the typewritten report translated him mentally to the luxurious chambers in Piccadilly.

Again, almost clairvoyantly, he saw the stoical American seated before the empty fireplace, his foot restlessly tapping the fender. Again he heard the curious, high tones: "I'll tell you . . . You have opened the gates of hell. . . ."

The whole scene, with its tantalizing undercurrent of mystery, was reenacted before his inner vision. He seemed to hear Nicol Brinn, startled from his reverie, exclaim: "I think it was an owl. . . . We sometimes get them over from the Green Park. . . ."

Why should so simple an incident have produced so singular an effect? For the face of the speaker had been ashen.

Then the pendulum swung inevitably back: "You are all perfectly cruel and horrible. . . ."

Paul Harley clenched his hands, frowning at the Burmese cabinet as though he hated it.

How persistently the voice of Phil Abingdon rang in his ears! He could not forget her lightest words. How hopelessly her bewitching image intruded itself between his reasoning mind and the problem upon which he sought to concentrate.

Miss Smith, the typist, had gone, for it was after six o'clock, and Innes alone was on duty. He came in as Harley, placing his hat and cane upon the big writing table, sat down to study the report.

"Inspector Wessex rang up, Mr. Harley, about an hour ago. He said he would be at the Yard until six."

"Has he obtained any information?" asked Paul Harley, wearily, glancing at his little table clock.

"He said he had had insufficient time to do much in the matter, but that there were one or two outstanding facts which might interest you."

"Did he seem to be surprised?"

"He did," confessed Innes. "He said that Ormuz Khan was a well-known figure in financial circles, and asked me in what way you were interested in him."

"Ah!" murmured Harley. He took up the telephone. "City 400," he said. . . . "Is that the Commissioner's Office, New Scotland Yard? . . . Paul Harley speaking. Would you please inquire if Detective Inspector Wessex has gone?"

While awaiting a reply he looked up at Innes. "Is there anything else?" he asked.

"Only the letters, Mr. Harley."

"No callers?"

"No."

"Leave the letters, then; I will see to them. You need not wait." A moment later, as his secretary bade him good-night and went out of the office:

"Hello," said Harley, speaking into the mouthpiece . . . "The inspector has gone? Perhaps you would ask him to ring me up in the morning." He replaced the receiver on the hook.

Resting his chin in his hands, he began to read from the typewritten pages before him. His assistant's report was conceived as follows:

Re Mr. Nicol Brinn of Raleigh House, Piccadilly, W. I.
    Mr. Nicol Brinn is an American citizen, born at Cincinnati, Ohio, February 15, 1884. He is the son of John Nicolas Brinn of the same city, founder of the firm of J. Nicolas Brinn, Incorporated, later reconstituted under the style of Brinn's Universal Electric Supply Corporation.
    Nicol Brinn is a graduate of Harvard. He has travelled extensively in nearly all parts of the world and has access to the best society of Europe and America. He has a reputation for eccentricity, has won numerous sporting events as a gentleman rider; was the first airman to fly over the Rockies; took part in the Uruguay rebellion of 1904, and held the rank of lieutenant colonel of field artillery with the American forces during the Great War.

He has published a work on big game and has contributed numerous travel articles to American periodicals. On the death of Mr. Brinn, senior, in 1914, he inherited an enormous fortune and a preponderating influence in the B.U.E.S.C. He has never taken any active part in conduct of the concern, but has lived a restless and wandering life in various parts of the world.

Mr. Nicol Brinn is a confirmed bachelor. I have been unable to find that he has ever taken the slightest interest in any woman other than his mother throughout his career. Mrs. J. Nicolas Brinn is still living in Cincinnati, and there is said to be a strong bond of affection between mother and son. His movements on yesterday, 4th June, 1921, were as follows:

He came out of his chambers at eight o'clock and rode for an hour in the park, when he returned and remained indoors until midday. He then drove to the Carlton, where he lunched with the Foreign Secretary, with whom he remained engaged in earnest conversation until ten minutes to three. The Rt. Hon. gentleman proceeded to the House of Commons and Mr. Brinn to an auction at Christie's. He bought two oil paintings. He then returned to his chambers and did not reappear again until seven o'clock. He dined alone at a small and unfashionable restaurant in Soho, went on to his box at Covent Garden, where he remained for an hour, also alone, and then went home. He had no callers throughout the day.

Deliberately Paul Harley had read the report, only removing his hand from his chin to turn over the pages. Now from the cabinet at his elbow he took out his tin of tobacco and, filling and lighting a pipe, lay back, eyes half closed, considering what he had learned respecting Nicol Brinn.

That he was concerned in the death of Sir Charles Abingdon he did not believe for a moment; but that this elusive case, which upon investigation only seemed the more obscure, was nevertheless a case of deliberate murder he was as firmly convinced as ever. Of the identity of the murderer, of his motive, he had not the haziest idea, but that the cloud which he had pictured as overhanging the life of the late Sir Charles was a reality and not a myth of the imagination he became more completely convinced with each new failure to pick up a clue.

He found himself helplessly tied. In which direction should he move and to what end? Inclination prompted him in one direction, common sense held him back. As was his custom, he took a pencil and wrote upon a little block:

Find means to force Brinn to speak.

He lay back in his chair again, deep in thought, and presently added the note:

Obtain interview with Ormuz Khan.

Just as he replaced the pencil on the table, his telephone bell rang. The caller proved to be his friend, Inspector Wessex.

"Hello, Mr. Harley," said the inspector. "I had occasion to return to the Yard, and they told me you had rung up. I don't know why you are interested in this Ormuz Khan, unless you want to raise a loan."

Paul Harley laughed. "I gather that he is a man of extensive means," he replied, "but hitherto he has remained outside my radius of observation."

"And outside mine," declared the inspector. "He hasn't the most distant connection with anything crooked. It gave me a lot of trouble to find out what little I have found out. Briefly, all I have to tell you is this: Ormuz Khan—who is apparently entitled to be addressed as 'his excellency'—is a director of the Imperial Bank of Iran, and is associated, too, with one of the Ottoman banks. I presume his nationality is Persian, but I can't be sure of it. He periodically turns up in the various big capitals when international loans and that sort of thing are being negotiated. I understand that he has a flat somewhere in Paris, and the *Service de Sureté* tells me that his name is good for several million francs over there. He appears to have a certain fondness for London during the spring and early summer months, and I am told he has a fine place in Surrey. He is at present living at Savoy Court. He appears to be something of a dandy and to be very partial to the fair sex, but nevertheless there is nothing wrong with his reputation, considering, I mean, that the man is a sort of Eastern multimillionaire."

"Ah!" said Harley, who had been listening eagerly. "Is that the extent of your information, Wessex?"

"That's it," replied Wessex, with a laugh. "I hope you'll find it useful, but I doubt it. He hasn't been picking pockets or anything, has he?"

"No," said Harley, shortly. "I don't apprehend that his excellency will ever appear in your province, Wessex. My interest in him is of a purely personal nature. Thanks for all the trouble you have taken."

Paul Harley began to pace the office. From a professional point of view the information was uninteresting enough, but from another point of view it had awakened again that impotent anger which he had too often experienced in these recent, strangely restless days.

At all costs he must see Ormuz Khan, although how he was to obtain access to this man who apparently never left his private apartments (if the day of his vigil at the Savoy had been a typical one) he failed to imagine.

Nevertheless, pausing at the table, he again took up his pencil, and to the note "Obtain interview with Ormuz Khan" he added the one word, underlined:

Tomorrow.

X

HIS EXCELLENCY ORMUZ KHAN

THE CITY CLOCKS were chiming the hour of ten on the following morning when a page from the Savoy approached the shop of Mr. Jarvis, bootmaker, which is situated at no great distance from the hotel. The impudent face of the small boy wore an expression of seriocomic fright as he pushed open the door and entered the shop.

Jarvis, the bootmaker, belonged to a rapidly disappearing class of British tradesmen. He buckled to no one, but took an artistic pride in his own handiwork, criticism from a layman merely provoking a scornful anger which had lost Jarvis many good customers.

He was engaged, at the moment of the page's entrance, in a little fitting room at the back of his cramped premises, but through the doorway the boy could see the red, bespectacled face with its fringe of bristling white beard, in which he detected all the tokens of brewing storm. He whistled softly in self-sympathy.

"Yes, sir," Jarvis was saying to an invisible patron, "it's a welcome sight to see a real Englishman walk into my shop nowadays. London isn't London, sir, since the war, and the Strand will never be the Strand again." He turned to his assistant, who stood beside him, bootjack in hand. "If he sends them back again," he directed, "tell him to go to one of the French firms in Regent Street who cater to dainty ladies." He positively snorted with indignation, while the page, listening, whistled again and looked down at the parcel which he carried.

"An unwelcome customer, Jarvis?" inquired the voice of the man in the fitting room.

"Quite unwelcome," said Jarvis. "I don't want him. I have more work than I know how to turn out. I wish he would go elsewhere. I wish—"

He paused. He had seen the page boy. The latter, having undone his parcel, was holding out a pair of elegant, fawn-coloured shoes.

"Great Moses!" breathed Jarvis. "He's had the cheek to send them back again!"

"His excellency—" began the page, when Jarvis snatched the shoes from his hand and hurled them to the other end of the shop. His white beard positively bristled.

"Tell his excellency," he shouted, "to go to the devil, with my compliments!"

So positively ferocious was his aspect that the boy, with upraised arm, backed hastily out into the street. Safety won: "Blimey!" exclaimed the youth. "He's the warm goods, he is!"

He paused for several moments, staring in a kind of stupefied admiration at the closed door of Mr. Jarvis's establishment. He whistled again, softly, and then began to run—for the formidable Mr. Jarvis suddenly opened the door. "Hi, boy!" he called to the page. The page hesitated, glancing back doubtfully. "Tell his excellency that I will send round in about half an hour to remeasure his foot."

"D'you mean it?" inquired the boy, impudently—"or is there a catch in it?"

"I'll tan your hide, my lad!" cried the bootmaker—"and I mean that! Take my message and keep your mouth shut."

The boy departed, grinning, and little more than half an hour later a respectable-looking man presented himself at Savoy Court, inquiring of the attendant near the elevator for the apartments of "his excellency," followed by an unintelligible word which presumably represented "Ormuz Khan." The visitor wore a well-brushed but threadbare tweed suit, although his soft collar was by no means clean. He had a short, reddish-brown beard, and very thick, curling hair of the same hue protruded from beneath a bowler hat which had seen long service.

Like Mr. Jarvis, he was bespectacled, and his teeth were much discoloured and apparently broken in front, as is usual with cobblers. His hands, too, were toil-stained and his nails very black. He carried a cardboard box. He seemed to be extremely nervous, and this nervousness palpably increased when the impudent page, who was standing in the lobby, giggled on hearing his inquiry.

"He's second floor," said the youth. "Are you from Hot-Stuff Jarvis?"

"That's right, lad," replied the visitor, speaking with a marked Manchester accent. "From Mr. Jarvis."

"And are you really going up?" inquired the boy with mock solicitude.

"I'm going up right enough. That's what I'm here for."

"Shut up, Chivers," snapped the hall porter "Ring the bell." He glanced at the cobbler. "Second floor," he said, tersely, and resumed his study of a newspaper which he had been reading.

The representative of Mr. Jarvis was carried up to the second floor and the lift man, having indicated at which door he should knock, descended again. The cobbler's nervousness thereupon became more marked than ever, so that a waiter, seeing him looking helplessly from door to door, took pity on him and inquired for whom he was searching.

"His excellency," was the reply. "But I'm hanged if I can remember the number or how to pronounce his name."

The waiter glanced at him oddly. "Ormuz Khan," he said, and rang the bell beside a door. As he hurried away, "Good luck!" he called back.

There was a short interval, and then the door was opened by a man who looked like a Hindu. He wore correct morning dress and through gold-rimmed pince-nez he stared inquiringly at the caller.

"Is his excellency at home?" asked the latter. "I'm from Mr. Jarvis, the bootmaker."

"Oh!" said the other, smiling slightly. "Come in. What is your name?"

"Parker, sir. From Mr. Jarvis."

As the door closed, Parker found himself in a small lobby. Beside an umbrella rack a high-backed chair was placed. "Sit down," he was directed. "I will tell his excellency that you are here."

A door was opened and closed again, and Parker found himself alone. He twirled his bowler hat, which he held in his hand, and stared about the place vacantly. Once he began to whistle, but checked himself and coughed nervously. Finally the Hindu gentleman reappeared, beckoning to him to enter.

Parker stood up very quickly and advanced, hat in hand.

Then he remembered the box which he had left on the floor, and, stooping to recover it, he dropped his hat. But at last, leaving his hat upon the chair and carrying the box under his arm, he entered a room which had been converted into a very businesslike office.

There was a typewriter upon a table near the window at which someone had evidently been at work quite recently, and upon a larger table in the centre of the room were dispatch boxes, neat parcels of documents, ledgers, works of reference, and all the evidence of keen commercial activity. Crossing the room, the Hindu rapped upon an inner door, opened it, and standing aside, "The man from the bootmaker," he said in a low voice.

Parker advanced, peering about him as one unfamiliar with his surroundings. As he crossed the threshold the door was closed behind him, and he found himself in a superheated atmosphere heavy with the perfume of hyacinths.

The place was furnished as a sitting room, but some of its appointments were obviously importations. Its keynote was Orientalism, not of that sensuous yet grossly masculine character which surrounds the wealthy Eastern esthete but quite markedly feminine. There were an extraordinary number of cushions, and many bowls and vases containing hyacinths. What other strange appointments were present Parker was far too nervous to observe.

He stood dumbly before a man who lolled back in a deep, cushioned chair and whose almond-shaped eyes, black as night, were set immovably upon him. This man was apparently young. He wore a rich, brocaded robe, trimmed with marten, fur, and out of it his long ivory throat rose statuesquely. His complexion was likewise of this uniform ivory colour, and from his low smooth brow his hair was brushed back in a series of glossy black waves.

His lips were full and very red. As a woman he might have been considered handsome—even beautiful; in a man this beauty was unnatural and repellent. He wore Oriental slippers, fur-lined, and his feet rested on a small ottoman. One long, slender hand lay upon a cushion placed on the chair arm, and a pretty girl was busily engaged in manicuring his excellency's nails. Although the day held every promise of being uncomfortably hot, already a huge fire was burning in the grate.

As Parker stood before him, the languid, handsome Oriental did not stir a muscle, merely keeping the gaze of his strange black eyes fixed upon the nervous cobbler. The manicurist, after one quick upward glance, continued her work. But in this moment of distraction she had hurt the cuticle of one of those delicate, slender fingers.

Ormuz Khan withdrew his hand sharply from the cushion, glanced aside at the girl, and then, extending his hand again, pushed her away from him. Because of her half-kneeling posture, she almost fell, but managed to recover herself by clutching at the edge of a little table upon which the implements of her trade were spread. The table rocked and a bowl of water fell crashing on the carpet. His excellency spoke. His voice was very musical.

"Clumsy fool," he said. "You have hurt me. Go."

The girl became very white and began to gather up the articles upon the table. "I am sorry," she said, "but—"

"I do not wish you to speak," continued the musical voice. "Only to go."

Hurriedly collecting the remainder of the implements and placing them in an attache case, the manicurist hurried from the room. Her eyes were over-bright and her lips pathetically tremulous. Ormuz Khan never glanced in her direction again, but resumed his disconcerting survey of Parker. "Yes?" he said.

Parker bumblingly began to remove the lid of the cardboard box which he had brought with him.

"I do not wish you to alter the shoes you have made," said his excellency. "I instructed you to remeasure my foot in order that you might make a pair to fit."

"Yes, sir," said Parker. "Quite so, your excellency." And he dropped the box and the shoes upon the floor. "Just a moment, sir?"

From an inner pocket he drew out a large sheet of white paper, a pencil, and a tape measure. "Will you place your foot upon this sheet of paper, sir?"

Ormuz Khan raised his right foot listlessly.

"Slipper off, please, sir."

"I am waiting," replied the other, never removing his gaze from Parker's face.

"Oh, I beg your pardon sir, your excellency," muttered the bootmaker.

Dropping upon one knee, he removed the furred slipper from a slender, arched foot, bare, of the delicate colour of ivory, and as small as a woman's.

"Now, sir."

The ivory foot was placed upon the sheet of paper, and very clumsily Parker drew its outline. He then took certain measurements and made a number of notes with a stub of thick pencil. Whenever his none too clean hands touched Ormuz Khan's delicate skin the Oriental perceptibly shuddered.

"Of course, sir," said Parker at last, "I should really have taken your measurement with the sock on."

"I wear only the finest silk."

"Very well, sir. As you wish."

Parker replaced paper, pencil, and measure, and, packing up the rejected shoes, made for the door.

"Oh, bootmaker!" came the musical voice.

Parker turned. "Yes, sir?"

"They will be ready by Monday?"

"If possible, your excellency."

"Otherwise I shall not accept them."

Ormuz Khan drew a hyacinth from a vase close beside him and languidly waved it in dismissal.

In the outer room the courteous secretary awaited Parker, and there was apparently no one else in the place, for the Hindu conducted him to the lobby and opened the door.

Parker said "Good morning, sir," and would have departed without his hat had not the secretary smilingly handed it to him.

When, presently, the cobbler emerged from the elevator, below, he paused before leaving the hotel to mop his perspiring brow with a large, soiled handkerchief. The perfume of hyacinths seemed to have pursued him, bringing with it a memory of the handsome, effeminate ivory face of the man above. He was recalled to his senses by the voice of the impudent page.

"Been kicked out, gov'nor?" the youth inquired. "You're the third this morning."

"Is that so?" answered Parker. "Who were the other two, lad?"

"The girl wot comes to do his nails. A stunnin' bird, too. She came down cryin' a few minutes ago. Then—"

"Shut up, Chivers!" cried the hall porter. "You're asking for the sack, and I'm the man to get it for you."

Chivers did not appear to be vastly perturbed by this prospect, and he grinned agreeably at Parker as the latter made his way out into the courtyard.

Any one sufficiently interested to have done so might have found matter for surprise had he followed that conscientious bootmaker as he left the hotel. He did not proceed to the shop of Mr. Jarvis, but, crossing the Strand, mounted a city-bound motor bus and proceeded eastward upon it as far as the Law Courts. Here he dismounted and plunged into that maze of tortuous lanes which dissects the triangle formed by Chancery Lane and Holborn.

His step was leisurely, and once he stopped to light his pipe, peering with interest into the shop window of a law stationer. Finally he came to another little shop which had once formed part of a private house. It was of the lock-up variety, and upon the gauze blind which concealed the interior appeared the words: "The Chancery Agency."

Whether the Chancery Agency was a press agency, a literary or a dramatic agency, was not specified, but Mr. Parker was evidently well acquainted with the establishment, for he unlocked the door with a key which he carried and, entering a tiny shop, closed and locked the door behind him again.

The place was not more than ten yards square and the ceiling was very low. It was barely furnished as an office, but evidently Mr. Parker's business was not of a nature to detain him here. There was a second door to be unlocked; and beyond it appeared a flight of narrow stairs—at some time the servant's stair of the partially demolished house which had occupied that site in former days. Relocking this door in turn, Mr. Parker mounted the stair and presently found himself in a spacious and well-furnished bedroom.

This bedroom contained an extraordinary number of wardrobes, and a big dressing table with wing mirrors lent a theatrical touch to the apartment. This was still further enhanced by the presence of all sorts of wigs, boxes of false hair, and other items of make-up. At the table Mr. Parker seated himself, and when, half an hour later, the bedroom door was opened, it was not Mr. Parker who crossed the book-lined study within and walked through to the private office where Innes was seated writing. It was Mr. Paul Harley.

XI

THE PURPLE STAIN

FOR MORE THAN an hour Harley sat alone, smoking, neglectful of the routine duties which should have claimed his attention. His face was set and grim, and his expression one of total abstraction. In spirit he stood again in that superheated room at the Savoy. Sometimes, as he mused, he would smoke with unconscious vigour, surrounding himself with veritable fog banks. An imaginary breath of hyacinths would have reached him, to conjure up vividly the hateful, perfumed environment of Ormuz Khan.

He was savagely aware of a great mental disorderliness. He recognized that his brain remained a mere whirlpool from which Phyllis Abingdon, the deceased Sir Charles, Nicol Brinn, and another, alternately arose to claim supremacy. He clenched his teeth upon the mouthpiece of his pipe.

But after some time, although rebelliously, his thoughts began to marshal themselves in a certain definite formation. And outstanding, alone, removed from the ordinary, almost from the real, was the bizarre personality of Ormuz Khan.

The data concerning the Oriental visitor, as supplied by Inspector Wessex, had led him to expect quite a different type of character. Inured as Paul Harley was to surprise, his first sentiment as he had set eyes upon the man had been one of sheer amazement.

"Something of a dandy," inadequately described the repellent sensuousness of this veritable potentate, who could contrive to invest a sitting room in a modern hotel with the atmosphere of a secret Eastern household. To consider Ormuz Khan in connection with matters of international finance was wildly incongruous, while the manicurist incident indicated an inherent cruelty only possible in one of Oriental race.

In a mood of complete mental detachment Paul Harley found himself looking again into those black, inscrutable eyes and trying to analyze the elusive quality of their regard. They were unlike any eyes that he had met with. It were folly to count their possessor a negligible quantity. Nevertheless, it was difficult, because of the fellow's scented effeminacy, to believe that women could find him attractive. But Harley, wise in worldly lore, perceived that the mystery surrounding Ormuz Khan must make a strong appeal to a certain type of female mind. He was forced to admit that some women, indeed many, would be as clay in the hands of the man who possessed those long-lashed, magnetic eyes.

He thought of the pretty manicurist. Mortification he had read in her white face, and pain; but no anger. Yes, Ormuz Khan was dangerous.

In what respect was he dangerous?

"Phil Abingdon!" Harley whispered, and, in the act of breathing the name, laughed at his own folly.

In the name of reason, he mused, what could she find to interest her in a man of Ormuz Khan's type? He was prepared to learn that there was a mystic side to her personality—a phase in her character which would be responsive to the outre and romantic. But he was loath to admit that she could have any place in her affections for the scented devotee of hyacinths.

Thus, as always, his musings brought him back to the same point. He suppressed a groan and, standing up, began to pace the room. To and fro he walked, before the gleaming cabinet, and presently his expression underwent a subtle change. His pipe had long since gone out, but he had failed to observe the fact. His eyes had grown unusually bright—and suddenly he stepped to the table and stooping made a note upon the little writing block.

He rang the bell communicating with the outer office. Innes came in. "Innes," he said, rapidly, "is there anything of really first-rate importance with which I should deal personally?"

"Well," replied the secretary, glancing at some papers which he carried, "there is nothing that could not wait until tomorrow at a pinch."

"The pinch has come," said Harley. "I am going to interview the two most important witnesses in the Abingdon case."

"To whom do you refer, Mr. Harley?"

Innes stared rather blankly, as he made the inquiry, whereupon:

"I have no time to explain," continued Harley. "But I have suddenly realized the importance of a seemingly trivial incident which I witnessed. It is these trivial incidents, Innes, which so often contain the hidden clue."

"What! you really think you have a clue at last?"

"I do." The speaker's face grew grimly serious. "Innes, if I am right, I shall probably proceed to one of two places: the apartments of Ormuz Khan or the chambers of Nicol Brinn. Listen. Remain here until I phone—whatever the hour."

"Shall I advise Wessex to stand by?"

Harley nodded. "Yes—do so. You understand, Innes, I am engaged and not to be disturbed on any account?"

"I understand. You are going out by the private exit?"

"Exactly."

As Innes retired, quietly closing the door, Harley took up the telephone and called Sir Charles Abingdon's number. He was answered by a voice which he recognized.

"This is Paul Harley speaking," he said. "Is that Benson?"

"Yes, sir," answered the butler. "Good morning, sir."

"Good morning, Benson. I have one or two questions to ask you, and there is something I want you to do for me. Miss Abingdon is out, I presume?"

"Yes, sir," replied Benson, sadly. "At the funeral, sir."

"Is Mrs. Howett in?"

"She is, sir."

"I shall be around in about a quarter of an hour, Benson. In the meantime, will you be good enough to lay the dining table exactly as it was laid on the night of Sir Charles's death?"

Benson could be heard nervously clearing his throat, then: "Perhaps, sir," he said, diffidently, "I didn't quite understand you. Lay the table, sir, for dinner?"

"For dinner—exactly. I want everything to be there that was present on the night of the tragedy; everything. Naturally you will have to place different flowers in the vases, but I want to see the same vases. From the soup tureen to the serviette rings, Benson, I wish you to duplicate the dinner table as I remember it, paying particular attention to the exact position of each article. Mrs. Howett will doubtless be able to assist you in this."

"Very good, sir," said Benson—but his voice betokened bewilderment. "I will see Mrs. Howett at once, sir."

"Right. Good-bye."

"Good-bye, sir."

Replacing the receiver, Harley took a bunch of keys from his pocket and, crossing the office, locked the door. He then retired to his private apartments and also locked the communicating door. A few moments later he came out of "The Chancery Agency" and proceeded in the direction of the Strand. Under cover of the wire-gauze curtain which veiled the window he had carefully inspected the scene before emerging. But although his eyes were keen and his sixth sense whispered "Danger-danger!" he had failed to detect anything amiss.

This constant conflict between intuition and tangible evidence was beginning to tell upon him. Either his sixth sense had begun to play tricks or he was the object of the most perfectly organized and efficient system of surveillance with which he had ever come in contact. Once, in the past, he had found himself pitted against the secret police of Moscow, and hitherto he had counted their methods incomparable. Unless he was the victim of an unpleasant hallucination, those Russian spies had their peers in London.

As he alighted from a cab before the house of the late Sir Charles, Benson opened the door. "We have just finished, sir," he said, as Harley ran up the steps. "But Mrs. Howett would like to see you, sir."

"Very good, Benson," replied Harley, handing his hat and cane to the butler. "I will see her in the dining room, please."

Benson throwing open the door, Paul Harley walked into the room which so often figured in his vain imaginings. The table was laid for dinner in accordance with his directions. The chair which he remembered to have occupied was in place and that in which Sir Charles had died was set at the head of the table.

Brows contracted, Harley stood just inside the room, looking slowly about him. And, as he stood so, an interrogatory cough drew his gaze to the doorway. He turned sharply, and there was Mrs. Howett, a pathetic little figure in black.

"Ah, Mrs. Howett," said Harley; kindly, "please try to forgive me for this unpleasant farce with its painful memories. But I have a good reason. I think you know this. Now, as I am naturally anxious to have everything clear before Miss Abingdon returns, will you be good enough to tell me if the table is at present set exactly as on the night that Sir Charles and I came in to dinner?"

"No, Mr. Harley," was the answer, "that was what I was anxious to explain. The table is now laid as Benson left it on that dreadful night."

"Ah, I see. Then you, personally, made some modifications?"

"I rearranged the flowers and moved the centre vase so." The methodical old lady illustrated her words. "I also had the dessert spoons changed. You remember, Benson?"

Benson inclined his head. From a sideboard he took out two silver spoons which he substituted for those already set upon the table.

"Anything else, Mrs. Howett?"

"The table is now as I left it, sir, a few minutes before your arrival. Just after your arrival I found Jones, the parlourmaid—a most incompetent, impudent girl—altering the position of the serviettes. At least, such was my impression."

"Of the serviettes?" murmured Harley.

"She denied it," continued the housekeeper, speaking with great animation, "but she could give no explanation. It was the last straw. She took too many liberties altogether."

As Harley remained silent, the old lady ran on animatedly, but Harley was no longer listening.

"This is not the same table linen?" he asked, suddenly.

"Why, no, sir," replied Benson. "Last week's linen will be at the laundry."

"It has not gone yet," interrupted Mrs. Howett. "I was making up the list when you brought me Mr. Harley's message."

Paul Harley turned to her.

"May I ask you to bring the actual linen used at table on that occasion, Mrs. Howett?" he said. "My request must appear singular, I know, but I assure you it is no idle one."

Benson looked positively stupid, but Mrs. Howett, who had conceived a sort of reverence for Paul Harley, hurried away excitedly.

"Finally, Benson," said Harley, "what else did you bring into the room after Sir Charles and I had entered?"

"Soup, sir. Here is the tureen, on the sideboard, and all the soup plates of the service in use that night. Of course, sir, I can't say which were the actual plates used."

Paul Harley inspected the plates, a set of fine old Derby ware, and gazed meditatively at the silver ladle. "Did the maid, Jones, handle any of these?" he asked.

"No, sir"—emphatically. "She was preparing to bring the trout from the kitchen."

"But I saw her in the room."

"She had brought in the fish plates, a sauce boat, and two toast racks, sir. She put them here, on the sideboard. But they were never brought to the table."

"H'm. Has Jones left?"

"Yes, sir. She was under notice. But after her rudeness, Mrs. Howett packed her off right away. She left the very next day after poor Sir Charles died."

"Where has she gone?"

"To a married sister, I believe, until she finds a new job. Mrs. Howett has the address."

At this moment Mrs. Howett entered, bearing a tablecloth and a number of serviettes.

"This was the cloth," she said, spreading it out, "but which of the serviettes were used I cannot say."

"Allow me to look," replied Paul Harley.

One by one he began to inspect the serviettes, opening each in turn and examining it critically.

"What have we here!" he exclaimed, presently. "Have blackberries been served within the week, Mrs. Howett?"

"We never had them on the table, Mr. Harley. Sir Charles—God rest him—said they irritated the stomach. Good gracious!" She turned to Benson. "How is it I never noticed those stains, and what can have caused them?"

The serviette which Paul Harley held outstretched was covered all over with dark purple spots.

XII

THE VEIL IS RAISED

RISING FROM THE writing table in the library, Paul Harley crossed to the mantelpiece and stared long and hungrily at a photograph in a silver frame. So closely did he concentrate upon it that he induced a sort of auto-hypnosis, so that Phil Abingdon seemed to smile at him sadly. Then a shadow appeared to obscure the piquant face. The soft outline changed, subtly; the lips grew more full, became voluptuous; the eyes lengthened and grew languorous. He found himself looking into the face of Ormuz Khan.

"Damn it!" he muttered, awakened from his trance.

He turned aside, conscious of a sudden, unaccountable chill. It might have been caused by the mental picture which he had conjured up, or it might be another of those mysterious warnings of which latterly he had had so many without encountering any positive danger. He stood quite still, listening.

Afterward he sometimes recalled that moment, and often enough asked himself what he had expected to hear. It was from this room, on an earlier occasion, that he had heard the ominous movements in the apartment above. Today he heard nothing.

"Benson," he called, opening the library door. As the man came along the hall: "I have written a note to Mr. Innes, my secretary," he explained. "There it is, on the table. When the district messenger, for whom you telephoned, arrives, give him the parcel and the note. He is to accept no other receipt than that of Mr. Innes."

"Very good, sir."

Harley took his hat and cane, and Benson opened the front door.

"Good day, sir," said the butler.

"Good day, Benson," called Harley, hurrying out to the waiting cab. "Number 236 South Lambeth Road," he directed the man.

Off moved the taxi, and Harley lay back upon the cushions heaving a long sigh. The irksome period of inaction was ended. The cloud which for a time had dulled his usually keen wits was lifted. He was by no means sure that enlightenment had come in time, but at least he was in hot pursuit of a tangible clue, and he must hope that it would lead him, though tardily, to the heart of this labyrinth which concealed—what?

Which concealed something, or someone, known and feared as Fire-Tongue.

For the moment he must focus upon establishing, beyond query or doubt, the fact that Sir Charles Abingdon had not died from natural causes. Premonitions, intuitions, beliefs resting upon a foundation of strange dreams—these were helpful to himself, if properly employed, but they were not legal evidence. This first point achieved, the motive of the crime must be sought; and then—the criminal.

"One thing at a time," Harley finally murmured.

Turning his head, he glanced back at the traffic in the street behind him. The action was sheerly automatic. He had ceased to expect to detect the presence of any pursuer. Yet he was convinced that his every movement was closely watched. It was uncanny, unnerving, this consciousness of invisible surveillance. Now, as he looked, he started. The invisible had become the visible.

His cab was just on the point of turning on to the slope of Vauxhall Bridge. And fifty yards behind, speeding along the Embankment, was a small French car. The features of the driver he had no time to observe. But, peering eagerly through the window, showed the dark face of the passenger. The man's nationality it was impossible to determine, but the keen, almost savage interest, betrayed by the glittering black eyes, it was equally impossible to mistake.

If the following car had turned on to the bridge, Harley, even yet, might have entertained a certain doubt. But, mentally putting himself in the pursuer's place, he imagined himself detected and knew at once exactly what he should do. Since this hypothetical course was actually pursued by the other, Harley's belief was confirmed.

Craning his neck, he saw the little French car turn abruptly and proceed in the direction of Victoria Station. Instantly he acted.

Leaning out of the window he thrust a ten-shilling note into the cabman's hand. "Slow down, but don't pull up," he directed. "I am going to jump out just as you pass that lorry ahead. Ten yards further on stop. Get down and crank your engine, and then proceed slowly over the bridge. I shall not want you again."

"Right-oh, sir," said the man, grinning broadly. As a result, immediately he was afforded the necessary cover, Harley jumped from the cab. The man reached back and closed the door, proceeding on his leisurely way. Excepting the driver of the lorry, no one witnessed this eccentric performance, and Harley, stepping on to the footpath, quietly joined the stream of pedestrians and strolled slowly along.

He presently passed the stationary cab without giving any sign of recognition to the dismounted driver. Then, a minute later, the cab overtook him and was soon lost in the traffic ahead. Even as it disappeared another cab went by rapidly.

Leaning forward in order to peer through the front window was the dark-faced man whom he had detected on the Embankment!

"Quite correct," murmured Harley, dryly. "Exactly what I should have done."

The spy, knowing himself discovered, had abandoned his own car in favour of a passing taxicab, and in the latter had taken up the pursuit.

Paul Harley lighted a cigarette. Oddly enough, he was aware of a feeling of great relief. In the first place, his sixth sense had been triumphantly vindicated; and, in the second place, his hitherto shadowy enemies, with their seemingly supernatural methods, had been unmasked. At least they were human, almost incredibly clever, but of no more than ordinary flesh and blood.

The contest had developed into open warfare. Harley's accurate knowledge of London had enabled him to locate No. 236 South Lambeth Road without recourse to a guide, and now, walking on past the big gas works and the railway station, he turned under the dark arches and pressed on to where a row of unprepossessing dwellings extended in uniform ugliness from a partly demolished building to a patch of waste ground.

That the house was being watched he did not doubt. In fact, he no longer believed subterfuge to be of any avail. He was dealing with dangerously accomplished criminals. How clever they were he had yet to learn; and it was only his keen intuitive which at this juncture enabled him to score a point over his cunning opponents.

He walked quite openly up the dilapidated steps to the door of No. 236, and was about to seize the dirty iron knocker when the door opened suddenly and a girl came out. She was dressed neatly and wore a pseudo fashionable hat from which a heavy figured veil depended so as almost to hide her features. She was carrying a bulging cane grip secured by a brown leather strap.

Seeing Harley on the step, she paused for a moment, then, recovering herself:

"Ellen!" she shouted down the dim passageway revealed by the opening of the door. "Somebody to see you."

Leaving the door open, she hurried past the visitor with averted face. It was well done, and, thus disguised by the thick veil, another man than Paul Harley might have failed to recognize one of whom he had never had more than an imperfect glimpse. But if Paul Harley's memory did not avail him greatly, his unerring instinct never failed.

He grasped the girl's arm. "One moment, Miss Jones," he said, quietly, "it is you I am here to see!"

The girl turned angrily, snatching her arm from his grasp. "You've made a mistake, haven't you?" she cried, furiously. "I don't know you and I don't want to!"

"Be good enough to step inside again. Don't make a scene. If you behave yourself, you have nothing to fear. But I want to talk to you."

He extended his arm to detain her. But she thrust it aside. "My boy's waiting round the corner!" she said, viciously. "Just see what he'll do when I tell him!"

"Step inside," repeated Harley, quietly. "Or accompany me to Kennington Lane Police Station—whichever you think would be the more amusing."

"What d'you mean!" blustered the girl. "You can't kid me. I haven't done anything."

"Then do as I tell you. You have got to answer my questions—either here or at the station. Which shall it be?"

He had realized the facts of the situation from the moment when the girl had made her sudden appearance, and he knew that his only chance of defeating his cunning opponents was to frighten her. Delicate measures would be wasted upon such a character. But even as the girl, flinging herself sullenly about, returned into the passage, he found himself admiring the resourcefulness of his unknown enemies.

A tired-looking woman carrying a child appeared from somewhere and stared apathetically at Harley.

Addressing the angry girl: "Another o' your flames, Polly?" she inquired in a dull voice. "Has he made you change your mind already?"

The girl addressed as "Polly" dropped her grip on the floor and, banging open a door, entered a shabby little sitting room, followed by Harley. Dropping onto a ragged couch, she stared obstinately out of the dirty window.

"Excuse me, madam, for intruding," said Harley to the woman with the baby, "but Polly has some information of use to the police. Oh, don't be alarmed. She has committed no crime. I shall only detain her for a few minutes."

He bowed to the tired-looking woman and closed the sitting-room door. "Now, young woman," he said, sternly, adopting this official manner of his friend, Inspector Wessex, "I am going to give you one warning, and one only. Although I don't think you know it, you have got mixed up with a gang of crooks. Play the game with me, and I'll stand by you. Try any funny business and you'll go to jail."

The official manner had its effect. Miss Jones looked sharply across at the speaker. "I haven't done anything," she said, sullenly.

Paul Harley advanced and stood over her. "What about the trick with the serviettes at Sir Charles Abingdon's?" he asked, speaking the words in slow and deliberate fashion.

The shaft went home, but the girl possessed a stock of obstinate courage. "What about it?" she inquired, but her voice had changed.

"Who made you do it?"

"What's that to you?"

Paul Harley drew out his watch, glanced at the face, and returned the timepiece to his pocket. "I have warned you," he said. "In exactly three minutes' time I shall put you under arrest."

The girl suddenly lifted her veil and, raising her face, looked up at him. At last he had broken down her obstinate resistance. Already he had noted the coarse, elemental formation of her hands, and now, the veil removed, he saw that she belonged to a type of character often found in Wales and closely duplicated in certain parts of London. There was a curious flatness of feature and prominence of upper jaw singularly reminiscent of the primitive Briton. Withal the girl was not unprepossessing in her coarse way. Utter stupidity and dogged courage are the outstanding characteristics of this type. But fear of the law is strong within them.

"Don't arrest me," she said. "I'll tell you."

"Good. In the first place, then, where were you going when I came here?"

"To meet my boy at Vauxhall Station."

"What is his name?"

"I'm not going to tell you. What's he done?"

"He has done murder. What is his name?"

"My God!" whispered the girl, and her face blanched swiftly. "Murder! I—I can't tell you his name—"

"You mean you won't?"

She did not answer.

"He is a very dark man," continued Harley "with black eyes. He is a Hindu."

The girl stared straight before her, dumbly.

"Answer me!" shouted Harley.

"Yes—yes! He is a foreigner."

"A Hindu?"

"I think so."

"He was here five minutes ago?"

"Yes."

"Where was he going to take you?"

"I don't know. He said he could put me in a good job out of London. We had only ten minutes to catch the train. He's gone to get the tickets."

"Where did you meet him?"

"In the Green Park."

"When?"

"About a month ago."

"Was he going to marry you?"

"Yes."

"What did you do to the serviettes on the night Sir Charles died?"

"Oh, my God! I didn't do anything to hurt him—I didn't do anything to hurt him!"

"Answer me."

"Sidney—"

"Oh, he called himself Sidney, did he? It isn't his name. But go on."

"He asked me to get one of the serviettes, with the ring, and to lend it to him."

"You did this?"

"Yes. But he brought it back."

"When?"

"The afternoon—"

"Before Sir Charles's death? Yes. Go on. What did he tell you to do with this serviette?"

"It—was in a box. He said I was not to open the box until I put the serviette on the table, and that it had to be put by Sir Charles's plate. It had to be put there just before the meal began."

"What else?"

"I had to burn the box."

"Well?"

"That night I couldn't see how it was to be done. Benson had laid the dinner table and Mrs. Howett was pottering about. Then, when I thought I had my chance, Sir Charles sat down in the dining room and began to read. He was still there and I had the box hidden in the hall stand, all ready, when Sidneyr ang up."

"Rang you up?"

"Yes. We had arranged it. He said he was my brother. I had to tell him I couldn't do it."

"Yes!"

"He said: 'You must.' I told him Sir Charles was in the dining room, and he said: 'I'll get him away. Directly he goes, don't fail to do what I told you'."

"And then?"

"Another 'phone call came—for Sir Charles. I knew who it was, because I had told Sidney about the case Sir Charles was attending in the square. When Sir Charles went out, I changed the serviettes. Mrs. Howett found me in the dining room and played hell. But afterward I managed to burn the box in the kitchen. That's all I know. What harm was there?"

"Harm enough!" said Harley, grimly. "And now—what was it that 'Sidney' stole from Sir Charles's bureau in the study?"

The girl started and bit her lip convulsively. "It wasn't stealing," she muttered. "It wasn't worth anything."

"Answer me. What did he take?"

"He took nothing."

"For the last time: answer!"

"It wasn't Sidney who took it. I took it."

"You took what?"

"A paper."

"You mean that you stole Sir Charles's keys and opened his bureau?"

"There was no stealing. He was out and they were lying on his dressing table. Sidney had told me to do it the first time I got a chance."

"What had he told you to do?"

"To search through Sir Charles's papers and see if there was anything with the word 'Fire-Tongue' in it!"

"Ah!" exclaimed Harley, a note of suppressed triumph in his voice. "Go on."

"There was only one paper about it," continued the girl, now speaking rapidly, "or only one that I could find. I put the bureau straight again and took this paper to Sidney."

"But you must have read the paper?"

"Only a bit of it. When I came to the word 'Fire-Tongue,' I didn't read any more."

"What was it about—the part you did read?"

"The beginning was all about India. I couldn't understand it. I jumped a whole lot. I hadn't much time and I was afraid Mrs. Howett would find me. Then, further on, I came to 'Fire-Tongue'."

"But what did it say about 'Fire-Tongue'?"

"I couldn't make it out, sir. Oh, indeed I'm telling you the truth! It seemed to me that Fire-Tongue was some sort of mark."

"Mark?"

"Yes—a mark Sir Charles had seen in India, and then again in London—"

"In London! Where in London?"

"On someone's arm."

"What! Tell me the name of this person!"

"I can't remember, sir! Oh, truly I can't."

"Was the name mentioned?"

"Yes."

"Was it Armand?"

"No."

"Ormond?"

"No."

"Anything like Ormond?"

The girl shook her head.

"It was not Ormuz Khan?"

"No. I am sure it wasn't."

Paul Harley's expression underwent a sudden change. "Was it Brown?" he asked.

She hesitated. "I believe it did begin with a B." she admitted.

"Was it Brunn?"

"No! I remember, sir. It was Brinn!"

"Good God!" muttered Harley. "Are you sure?"

"Quite sure."

"Do you know any one of that name?"

"No, sir."

"And is this positively all you remember?"

"On my oath, it is."

"How often have you seen Sidney since your dismissal?"

"I saw him on the morning I left."

"And then not again until today?"

"No."

"Does he live in London?"

"No. He is a valet to a gentleman who lives in the country."

"How do you know?"

"He told me."

"What is the name of the place?"

"I don't know."

"Once again—what is the name of the place?"

The girl bit her lip.

"Answer!" shouted Harley.

"I swear, sir," cried the girl, beginning suddenly to sob, "that I don't know! Oh, please, let me go! I swear I have told you all I know!"

"Good!"

Paul Harley glanced at his watch, crossed the room, and opened the door. He turned. "You can go now," he said. "But I don't think you will find Sidney waiting!"

It wanted only three minutes to midnight, and Innes, rather haggard and anxious-eyed, was pacing Paul Harley's private office when the 'phone bell rang. Eagerly he took up the receiver.

"Hullo!" came a voice. "That you, Innes?"

"Mr. Harley!" cried Innes. "Thank God you are safe! I was growing desperately anxious!"

"I am by no means safe, Innes! I am in one of the tightest corners of my life! Listen: Get Wessex! If he's off duty, get Burton. Tell him to bring—"

The voice ceased.

"Hullo!—Mr. Harley!" called Innes. "Mr. Harley!"

A faint cry answered him. He distinctly heard the sound of a fall. Then the other receiver was replaced on the hook.

"Merciful Heavens!" whispered Innes. "What has happened? Where was he speaking from? What can I do?"

XIII

NICOL BRINN HAS A VISITOR

IT WAS CLOSE upon noon, but Nicol Brinn had not yet left his chambers. From that large window which overlooked Piccadilly he surveyed the prospect with dull, lack-lustre eyes. His morning attire was at least as tightly fitting as that which he favoured in the evening, and now, hands clasped behind his back and an unlighted cigar held firmly in the left corner of his mouth, he gazed across the park with a dreamy and vacant regard. One very familiar with this strange and taciturn man might have observed that his sallow features looked even more gaunt than usual. But for any trace of emotion in that stoic face the most expert physiognomist must have sought in vain.

Behind the motionless figure the Alaskan ermine and Manchurian leopards stared glassily across the room. The flying lemur continued apparently to contemplate the idea of swooping upon the head of the tigress where she crouched upon her near-by pedestal. The death masks grinned; the Egyptian priestess smiled. And Nicol Britain, expressionless, watched the traffic in Piccadilly.

There came a knock at the door.

"In," said Nicol Brinn.

Hoskins, his manservant, entered. "Detective Inspector Wessex would like to see you, sir."

Nicol Brinn did not turn around. "In," he repeated.

Silently Hoskins retired, and, following a short interval, ushered into the room a typical detective officer, a Scotland Yard man of the best type. For Detective Inspector Wessex no less an authority than Paul Harley had predicted a brilliant future, and since he had attained to his present rank while still a comparatively young man, the prophecy of the celebrated private investigator was likely to be realized. Nicol Brinn turned and bowed in the direction of a large armchair.

"Pray sit down, Inspector," he said.

The high, monotonous voice expressed neither surprise nor welcome, nor any other sentiment whatever.

Detective Inspector Wessex returned the bow, placed his bowler hat upon the carpet, and sat down in the armchair. Nicol Brinn seated himself upon a settee over which was draped a very fine piece of Persian tapestry, and stared at his visitor with eyes which expressed nothing but a sort of philosophic stupidity, but which, as a matter of fact, photographed the personality of the man indelibly upon that keen brain.

Detective Inspector Wessex cleared his throat and did not appear to be quite at ease.

"What is it?" inquired Nicol Brinn and proceeded to light his cigar.

"Well, sir," said the detective frankly, "it's a mighty awkward business, and I don't know just how to approach it."

"Shortest way," drawled Nicol Brinn. "Don't study me."

"Thanks," said Wessex, "I'll do my best. It's like this—" he stared frankly at the impassive face. "Where is Mr. Paul Harley?"

Nicol Brinn gazed at the lighted end of his cigar meditatively for a moment and then replaced it in the right and not in the left corner of his mouth. Even to the trained eye of the detective inspector, he seemed to be quite unmoved, but one who knew him well would have recognized that this simple action betokened suppressed excitement.

"He left these chambers at ten-fifteen on Wednesday night," replied the American. "I had never seen him before, and I have never seen him since."

"Sure?"

"Quite."

"Could you swear to it before a jury?"

"You seem to doubt my word."

Detective Inspector Wessex stood up. "Mr. Brinn," he said, "I am in an awkward corner. I know you for a man with a fine sporting reputation, and therefore I don't doubt your word. But Mr. Paul Harley disappeared last night."

At last Nicol Brinn was moved. A second time he took the cigar from his mouth, gazed at the end reflectively, and then hurled the cigar across the room into the hearth. He stood up, walked to a window, and stared out. "Just sit quiet a minute," came the toneless voice. "You've hit me harder than you know. I want to think it out."

At the back of the tall, slim figure Detective Inspector Wessex stared with a sort of wonder. Mr. Nicol Brinn of Cincinnati was a conundrum which he found himself unable to catalogue, although in his gallery of odd characters were many eccentrics. If Nicol Brinn should prove to be crooked, then automatically he became insane. This Wessex had reasoned out even before he had set eyes upon the celebrated American traveller. His very first glimpse of Nicol Brinn had confirmed his reasoning, except that the cool, calm strength of the man had done much to upset the theory of lunacy.

Followed an interval of unbroken silence. Not even the ticking of a clock could be heard in that long, singularly furnished apartment. Then, as the detective continued to gaze upon the back of Mr. Nicol Brinn, suddenly the latter turned.

"Detective Inspector Wessex," he said, "there has been a cloud hanging over my head for seven years. That cloud is going to burst very soon, and it looks as if it were going to do damage."

"I don't understand you, sir," replied the detective bluntly. "But I have been put in charge of the most extraordinary case that has ever come my way, and I'll ask you to make yourself as clear as possible."

"I'll do all I can," Nicol Brinn assured him. "But first tell me something: Why have you come to me for information in respect to Mr. Paul Harley?"

"I'll answer your question," said Wessex, and the fact did not escape the keen observing power of Nicol Brinn that the detective's manner had grown guarded. "He informed Mr. Innes, his secretary, before setting out, that he was coming here to your chambers."

Nicol Brinn stared blankly at the speaker. "He told him that? When?"

"Yesterday."

"That he was coming here?"

"He did."

Nicol Brinn sat down again upon the settee. "Detective Inspector," said he, "I give you my word of honour as a gentleman that I last saw Mr. Paul Harley at ten-fifteen on Wednesday night. Since then, not only have I not seen him, but I have received no communication from him."

The keen glance of the detective met and challenged the dull glance of the speaker.

"I accept your word, sir," said Wessex finally, and he sighed and scratched his chin in the manner of a man hopelessly puzzled.

Silence fell again. The muted sounds of Piccadilly became audible in the stillness. Cabs and cars rolled by below, their occupants all unaware of the fact that in that long, museumlike room above their heads lay the key to a tragedy and the clue to a mystery.

"Look here, sir," said the detective suddenly, "the result of Mr. Paul Harley's investigations right up to date has been placed in my hands, together with all his notes. I wonder if you realize the fact that, supposing Mr. Harley does not return, I am in repossession of sufficient evidence to justify me in putting you under arrest?"

"I see your point quite clearly," replied Nicol Brinn. "I have seen my danger since the evening that Mr Paul Harley walked into this room, but I did not anticipate this particular development."

"To get right down to business," said Wessex, "if Mr. Paul Harley did not come here, where, in your idea, did he go?"

Nicol Brinn considered the speaker meditatively. "If I knew that," said he, "maybe I could help. I told him here in this very room that the pair of us were walking on the edge of hell. I don't like to say it, and you don't know all it means, but in my opinion he has taken a step too far."

Detective Inspector Wessex stood up impatiently. "You have already talked in that strain to Mr. Harley," he said, a bit brusquely. "Mr. Innes has reported something of the conversation to me. But I must ask you to remember that, whereas Mr. Paul Harley is an unofficial investigator, I am an officer of the Criminal Investigation Department, and figures of speech are of no use to me. I want facts. I want plain speaking. I ask you for help and you answer in parables. Now perhaps I am saying too much, and perhaps I am not, but that Mr. Harley was right in what he believed, the circumstances of his present disappearance go to prove. He learned too much about something called Fire-Tongue."

Wessex spoke the word challengingly, staring straight into the eyes of Nicol Brinn, but the latter gave no sign, and Wessex, concealing his disappointment, continued: "You know more about Fire-Tongue than you ever told Mr. Paul Harley. All you know I have got to know. Mr. Harley has been kidnapped, perhaps done to death."

"Why do you say so?" asked Nicol Brinn, rapidly.

"Because I know it is so. It does not matter how I know."

"You are certain that his absence is not voluntary?"

"We have definite evidence to that effect."

"I don't expect you to be frank with me, Detective Inspector, but I'll be as frank with you as I can be. I haven't the slightest idea in the world where Mr. Harley is. But I have information which, if I knew where he was, would quite possibly enable me to rescue him."

"Provided he is alive!" added Wessex, angrily.

"What leads you to suppose that he is not?"

"If he is alive, he is a prisoner."

"Good God!" said Nicol Brinn in a low voice. "It has come." He took a step toward the detective. "Mr. Wessex," he continued, "I don't tell you to do whatever your duty indicates; I know you will do it. But in the interests of everybody concerned I have a request to make. Have me watched if you like—I suppose that's automatic. But whatever happens, and wherever your suspicions point, give me twenty-four hours. As I think you can see, I am a man who thinks slowly, but moves with a rush. You can believe me or not, but I am even more anxious than you are to see this thing through. You think I know what lies back of it all, and I don't say that you are not right. But one thing you don't know, and that thing I can't tell you. In twenty-four hours I might be able to tell you. Whatever happens, even if poor Harley is found dead, don't hamper my movements between now and this time tomorrow."

Wessex, who had been watching the speaker intently, suddenly held out his hand. "It's a bet!" he said. "It's my case, and I'll conduct it in my own way."

"Mr. Wessex," replied Nicol Brinn, taking the extended hand, "I think you are a clever man. There are questions you would like to ask me, and there are questions I would like to ask you. But we both realize the facts of the situation, and we are both silent. One thing I'll say: You are in the deadliest peril you have ever known. Be careful. Believe me I mean it. Be very careful."

XIV

WESSEX GETS BUSY

INNES ROSE FROM the chair usually occupied by Paul Harley as Detective Inspector Wessex, with a very blank face, walked into the office. Innes looked haggard and exhibited unmistakable signs of anxiety. Since he had received that dramatic telephone message from his chief he had not spared himself for a moment. The official machinery of Scotland Yard was at work endeavouring to trace the missing man, but since it had proved impossible to find out from where the message had been sent, the investigation was handicapped at the very outset. Close inquiries at the Savoy Hotel had shown that Harley had not been there. Wessex, who was a thorough artist within his limitations, had satisfied himself that none of the callers who had asked for Ormuz Khan, and no one who had loitered about the lobbies, could possibly have been even a disguised Paul Harley.

To Inspector Wessex the lines along which Paul Harley was operating remained a matter of profound amazement and mystification. His interview with Mr. Nicol Brinn had only served to baffle him more hopelessly than ever. The nature of Paul Harley's inquiries—inquiries which, presumably from the death of Sir Charles Abingdon, had led him to investigate the movements of two persons of international repute, neither apparently having even the most remote connection with anything crooked—was a conundrum for the answer to which the detective inspector sought in vain.

"I can see you have no news," said Innes, dully.

"To be perfectly honest," replied Wessex, "I feel like a man who is walking in his sleep. Except for the extraordinary words uttered by the late Sir Charles Abingdon, I fail to see that there is any possible connection between his death and Mr. Nicol Brinn. I simply can't fathom what Mr. Harley was working upon. To my mind there is not the slightest evidence of foul play in the case. There is no motive; apart from which, there is absolutely no link."

"Nevertheless," replied Innes, slowly, "you know the chief, and therefore you know as well as I do that he would not have instructed me to communicate with you unless he had definite evidence in his possession. It is perfectly clear that he was interrupted in the act of telephoning. He was literally dragged away from the instrument."

"I agree," said Wessex. "He had got into a tight corner somewhere right enough. But where does Nicol Brinn come in?"

"How did he receive your communication?"

"Oh, it took him fairly between the eyes. There is no denying that.

He knows something."

"What he knows," said Innes, slowly, "is what Mr. Harley learned last night, and what he fears is what has actually befallen the chief."

Detective Inspector Wessex stood beside the Burmese cabinet, restlessly drumming his fingers upon its lacquered surface. "I am grateful for one thing," he said. "The press has not got hold of this story."

"They need never get hold of it if you are moderately careful."

"For several reasons I am going to be more than moderately careful. Whatever Fire-Tongue may be, its other name is sudden death! It's a devil of a business; a perfect nightmare. But—" he paused.

"I am wondering what on earth induced Mr. Harley to send that parcel of linen to the analyst."

"The result of the analysis may prove that the chief was not engaged upon any wild-goose chase."

"By heavens!" Wessex sprang up, his eyes brightened, and he reached for his hat, "that gives me an idea!"

"The message with the parcel was written upon paper bearing the letterhead of the late Sir Charles Abingdon. So Mr. Harley evidently made his first call there! I'm off, sir! The trail starts from that house!"

Leaving Innes seated at the big table with an expression of despair upon his face, Detective Inspector Wessex set out. He blamed himself for wasting time upon the obvious, for concentrating too closely upon the clue given by Harley's last words to Innes before leaving the office in Chancery Lane. It was poor workmanship. He had hoped to take a short cut, and it had proved, as usual, to be a long one. Now, as he sat in a laggard cab feeling that every minute wasted might be a matter of life and death, he suddenly became conscious of personal anxiety. He was a courageous, indeed a fearless, man, and he was subconsciously surprised to find himself repeating the words of Nicol Brinn: "Be careful—be very careful!" With all the ardour of the professional, he longed to find a clue which should lead him to the heart of the mystery.

Innes had frankly outlined the whole of Paul Harley's case to date, and Detective Inspector Wessex, although he had not admitted the fact, had nevertheless recognized that from start to finish the thing did not offer one single line of inquiry which he would have been capable of following up. That Paul Harley had found material to work upon, had somehow picked up a definite clue from this cloudy maze, earned the envious admiration of the Scotland Yard man.

Arrived at his destination, he asked to see Miss Abingdon, and was shown by the butler into a charmingly furnished little sitting room which was deeply impressed with the personality of its dainty owner. It was essentially and delightfully feminine. Yet in the decorations and in the arrangement of the furniture there was a note of independence which was almost a note of defiance. Phyllis Abingdon, an appealingly pathetic figure in her black dress, rose to greet the inspector.

"Don't be alarmed, Miss Abingdon," he said, kindly. "My visit does not concern you personally in any way, but I thought perhaps you might be able to help me trace Mr. Paul Harley."

Wessex had thus expressed himself with the best intentions, but even before the words were fully spoken he realized with a sort of shock that he could not well have made a worse opening. Phil Abingdon's eyes seemed to grow alarmingly large. She stood quite still, twisting his card between her supple fingers.

"Mr. Harley!" she whispered.

"I did not want to alarm you," said the detective, guiltily, "but—" He stopped, at a loss for words.

"Has something happened to him?"

"I am sorry if I have alarmed you," he assured her, "but there is some doubt respecting Mr. Harley's present whereabouts. Have you any idea where he went when he left this house yesterday?"

"Yes, yes. I know where he went, quite well."

"Benson, the butler, told me all about it when I came in." Phil Abingdon spoke excitedly, and took a step nearer Wessex. "He went to call upon Jones, our late parlourmaid."

"Late parlourmaid?" echoed Wessex, uncomprehendingly.

"Yes. He seemed to think he had made a discovery of importance."

"Something to do with a parcel which he sent away from here to the analyst?"

"Yes! I have been wondering whatever it could be. In fact, I rang up his office this morning, but learned that he was out. It was a serviette which he took away. Did you know that?"

"I did know it, Miss Abingdon. I called upon the analyst. I understand you were out when Mr. Harley came. May I ask who interviewed him?"

"He saw Benson and Mrs. Howett, the housekeeper."

"May I also see them?"

"Yes, with pleasure. But please tell me"—Phil Abingdon looked up at him pleadingly—"do you think something—something dreadful has happened to Mr. Harley?"

"Don't alarm yourself unduly," said Wessex. "I hope before the day is over to be in touch with him."

As a matter of fact, he had no such hope. It was a lie intended to console the girl, to whom the news of Harley's disappearance seemed to have come as a terrible blow. More and more Wessex found himself to be groping in the dark. And when, in response to the ringing of the bell, Benson came in and repeated what had taken place on the previous day, the detective's state of mystification grew even more profound. As a matter of routine rather than with any hope of learning anything useful, he interviewed Mrs. Howett; but the statement of the voluble old lady gave no clue which Wessex could perceive to possess the slightest value.

Both witnesses having been dismissed, he turned again to Phil Abingdon, who had been sitting watching him with a pathetic light of hope in her eyes throughout his examination of the butler and Mrs. Howett.

"The next step is clear enough," he said, brightly. "I am off to South Lambeth Road. The woman Jones is the link we are looking for."

"But the link with what, Mr. Wessex?" asked Phil Abingdon. "What is it all about?—what does it all mean?"

"The link with Mr. Paul Harley," replied Wessex. He moved toward the door.

"But won't you tell me something more before you go?" said the girl, beseechingly. "I—I—feel responsible if anything has happened to Mr. Harley. Please be frank with me. Are you afraid he is—in danger?"

"Well, miss," replied the detective, haltingly, "he rang up his secretary, Mr. Innes, last night—we don't know where from—and admitted that he was in a rather tight corner. I don't believe for a moment that he is in actual danger, but he probably has"—again he hesitated—"good reasons of his own for remaining absent at present."

Phil Abingdon looked at him doubtingly. "I am almost afraid to ask you," she said in a low voice, "but—if you hear anything, will you ring me up?"

"I promise to do so."

Chartering a more promising-looking cab than that in which he had come, Detective Inspector Wessex proceeded to 236 South Lambeth Road. He had knocked several times before the door was opened by the woman to whom the girl Jones had called on the occasion of Harley's visit.

"I am a police officer," said the detective inspector, "and I have called to see a woman named Jones, formerly in the employ of Sir Charles Abingdon."

"Polly's gone," was the toneless reply.

"Gone? Gone where?"

"She went away last night to a job in the country."

"What time last night?"

"I can't remember the time. Just after a gentleman had called here to see her."

"Someone from the police?"

"I don't know. She seemed to be very frightened."

"Were you present when he interviewed her?"

"No."

"After he had gone, what did Polly do?"

"Sat and cried for about half an hour, then Sidney came for her."

"Sidney?"

"Her boy—the latest one."

"Describe Sidney."

"A dark fellow, foreign."

"French—German?"

"No. A sort of Indian, like."

"Indian?" snapped Wessex. "What do you mean by Indian?"

"Very dark," replied the woman without emotion, swinging a baby she held to and fro in a methodical way which the detective found highly irritating.

"You mean a native of India?"

"Yes, I should think so. I never noticed him much. Polly has so many."

"How long has she known this man?"

"Only a month or so, but she is crazy about him."

"And when he came last night she went away with him?"

"Yes. She was all ready to go before the other gentleman called. He must have told her something which made her think it was all off, and she was crazy with joy when Sidney turned up. She had all her things packed, and off she went."

Experience had taught Detective Inspector Wessex to recognize the truth when he met it, and he did not doubt the statement of the woman with the baby. "Can you give me any idea where this man Sidney came from?" he asked.

"I am afraid I can't," replied the listless voice. "He was in the service of some gentleman in the country; that's all I know about him."

"Did Polly leave no address to which letters were to be forwarded?"

"No; she said she would write."

"One other point," said Wessex, and he looked hard into the woman's face: "What do you know about Fire-Tongue?"

He was answered by a stare of blank stupidity.

"You heard me?"

"Yes, I heard you, but I don't know what you are talking about."

Quick decisions are required from every member of the Criminal Investigation Department, and Detective Inspector Wessex came to one now.

"That will do for the present," he said, turned, and ran down the steps to the waiting cab.

XV

NAIDA

DUSK WAS FALLING that evening. Gaily lighted cars offering glimpses of women in elaborate toilets and of their black-coated and white-shirted cavaliers thronged Piccadilly, bound for theatre or restaurant. The workaday shutters were pulled down, and the night life of London had commenced. The West End was in possession of an army of pleasure seekers, but Nicol Brinn was not among their ranks. Wearing his tightly-buttoned dinner jacket, he stood, hands clasped behind him, staring out of the window as Detective Inspector Wessex had found him at noon. Only one who knew him very well could have detected the fact that anxiety was written upon that Sioux-like face. His gaze seemed to be directed, not so much upon the fading prospect of the park, as downward, upon the moving multitude in the street below. Came a subdued knocking at the door.

"In," said Nicol Brinn.

Hoskins, the neat manservant, entered. "A lady to see you, sir."

Nicol Brinn turned in a flash. For one fleeting instant the dynamic force beneath the placid surface exhibited itself in every line of his gaunt face. He was transfigured; he was a man of monstrous energy, of tremendous enthusiasm. Then the enthusiasm vanished. He was a creature of stone again; the familiar and taciturn Nicol Brinn, known and puzzled over in the club lands of the world.

"Name?"

"She gave none."

"English?"

"No, sir, a foreign lady."

"In."

Hoskins having retired, and having silently closed the door, Nicol Brinn did an extraordinary thing, a thing which none of his friends in London, Paris, or New York would ever have supposed him capable of doing. He raised his clenched hands. "Please God she has come," he whispered. "Dare I believe it? Dare I believe it?"

The door was opened again, and Hoskins, standing just inside, announced: "The lady to see you, sir."

He stepped aside and bowed as a tall, slender woman entered the room. She wore a long wrap trimmed with fur, the collar turned up about her face. Three steps forward she took and stopped. Hoskins withdrew and closed the door.

At that, while Nicol Brinn watched her with completely transfigured features, the woman allowed the cloak to slip from her shoulders, and, raising her head, extended both her hands, uttering a subdued cry of greeting that was almost a sob. She was dark, with the darkness of the East, but beautiful with a beauty that was tragic. Her eyes were glorious wells of sadness, seeming to mirror a soul that had known a hundred ages. Withal she had the figure of a girl, slender and supple, possessing the poetic grace and poetry of movement born only in the Orient.

"Naida!" breathed Nicol Brinn, huskily. "Naida!"

His high voice had softened, had grown tremulous. He extended his hands with a groping movement The woman laughed shudderingly.

Her cloak lying forgotten upon the carpet, she advanced toward him.

She wore a robe that was distinctly Oriental without being in the slightest degree barbaric. Her skin was strangely fair, and jewels sparkled upon her fingers. She conjured up dreams of the perfumed luxury of the East, and was a figure to fire the imagination. But Nicol Brinn seemed incapable of movement; his body was inert, but his eyes were on fire. Into the woman's face had come anxiety that was purely feminine.

"Oh, my big American sweetheart," she whispered, and, approaching him with a sort of timidity, laid her little hands upon his arm. "Do you still think I am beautiful?"

"Beautiful!"

No man could have recognized the voice of Nicol Brinn. Suddenly his arms were about her like bands of iron, and with a long, wondering sigh she lay back looking up into his face, while he gazed hungrily into her eyes. His lips had almost met hers when softly, almost inaudibly, she sighed: "Nicol!"

She pronounced the name queerly, giving to *i* the value of *ee*, and almost dropping the last letter entirely.

Their lips met, and for a moment they clung together, this woman of the East and man of the West, in utter transgression of that law which England's poet has laid down. It was a reunion speaking of a love so deep as to be sacred.

Lifting the woman in his arms lightly as a baby, he carried her to the settee between the two high windows and placed her there amid Oriental cushions, where she looked like an Eastern queen. He knelt at her feet and, holding both her hands, looked into her face with that wondering expression in which there was something incredulous and something sorrowful; a look of great and selfless tenderness. The face of Naida was lighted up, and her big eyes filled with tears. Disengaging one of her jeweled hands, she ruffled Nicol Brinn's hair.

"My Nicol," she said, tenderly. "Have I changed so much?"

Her accent was quaint and fascinating, but her voice was very musical. To the man who knelt at her feet it was the sweetest music in the world.

"Naida," he whispered. "Naida. Even yet I dare not believe that you are here."

"You knew I would come?"

"How was I to know that you would see my message?"

She opened her closed left hand and smoothed out a scrap of torn paper which she held there. It was from the "Agony" column of that day's *Times*.

N. November 23, 1913. N. B. See Telephone Directory.

"I told you long, long ago that I would come if ever you wanted me."

"Long, long ago," echoed Nicol Brinn. "To me it has seemed a century; tonight it seems a day."

He watched her with a deep and tireless content. Presently her eyes fell. "Sit here beside me," she said. "I have not long to be here. Put your arms round me. I have something to tell you."

He seated himself beside her on the settee, and held her close. "My Naida!" he breathed softly.

"Ah, no, no!" she entreated. "Do you want to break my heart?"

He suddenly released her, clenched his big hands, and stared down at the carpet. "You have broken mine."

Impulsively Naida threw her arms around his neck, coiling herself up lithely and characteristically beside him.

"My big sweetheart," she whispered, crooningly. "Don't say it—don't say it."

"I have said it. It is true."

Turning, fiercely he seized her. "I won't let you go!" he cried, and there was a strange light in his eyes. "Before I was helpless, now I am not. This time you have come to me, and you shall stay."

She shrank away from him terrified, wild-eyed. "Oh, you forget, you forget!"

"For seven years I have tried to forget. I have been mad, but tonight I am sane."

"I trusted you, I trusted you!" she moaned.

Nicol Brinn clenched his teeth grimly for a moment, and then, holding her averted face very close to his own, he began to speak in a low, monotonous voice. "For seven years," he said, "I have tried to die, because without you I did not care to live. I have gone into the bad lands of the world and into the worst spots of those bad lands. Night and day your eyes have watched me, and I have wakened from dreams of your kisses and gone out to court murder. I have earned the reputation of being something more than human, but I am not. I had everything that life could give me except you. Now I have got you, and I am going to keep you."

Naida began to weep silently. The low, even voice of Nicol Brinn ceased. He could feel her quivering in his grasp; and, as she sobbed, slowly, slowly the fierce light faded from his eyes.

"Naida, my Naida, forgive me," he whispered.

She raised her face, looking up to him pathetically. "I came to you, I came to you," she moaned. "I promised long ago that I would come. What use is it, all this? You know, you know! Kill me if you like. How often have I asked you to kill me. It would be sweet to die in your arms. But what use to talk so? You are in great danger or you would not have asked me to come. If you don't know it, I tell you—you are in great danger."

Nicol Brinn released her, stood up, and began slowly to pace about the room. He deliberately averted his gaze from the settee. "Something has happened," he began, "which has changed everything. Because you are here I know that—someone else is here."

He was answered by a shuddering sigh, but he did not glance in the direction of the settee.

"In India I respected what you told me. Because you were strong, I loved you the more. Here in England I can no longer respect the accomplice of assassins."

"Assassins? What, is this something new?"

"With a man's religion, however bloodthirsty it may be, I don't quarrel so long as he sincerely believes in it. But for private assassination I have no time and no sympathy." It was the old Nicol Brinn who was speaking, coldly and incisively. "That—something we both know about ever moved away from those Indian hills was a possibility I had never considered. When it was suddenly brought home to me that you, you, might be here in London, I almost went mad. But the thing that made me realize it was a horrible thing, a black, dastardly thing. See here."

He turned and crossed to where the woman was crouching, watching him with wide-open, fearful eyes. He took both her hands and looked grimly into her face. "For seven years I have walked around with a silent tongue and a broken heart. All that is finished. I am going to speak."

"Ah, no, no!" She was on her feet, her face a mask of tragedy. "You swore to me, you swore to me!"

"No oath holds good in the face of murder."

"Is that why you bring me here? Is that what your message means?"

"My message means that because of—the thing you know about—I am suspected of the murder."

"You? You?"

"Yes, I, I! Good God! when I realize what your presence here means, I wish more than ever that I had succeeded in finding death."

"Please don't say it," came a soft, pleading voice. "What can I do?

What do you want me to do?"

"I want you to release me from that vow made seven years ago."

Naida uttered a stifled cry. "How is it possible? You understand that it is not possible."

Nicol Brinn seized her by the shoulders. "Is it possible for me to remain silent while men are murdered here in a civilized country?"

"Oh," moaned Naida, "what can I do, what can I do?"

"Give me permission to speak and stay here. Leave the rest to me."

"You know I cannot stay, my Nicol," she replied, sadly.

"But," he said with deliberate slowness, "I won't let you go."

"You must let me go. Already I have been here too long."

He threw his arms around her and crushed her against him fiercely. "Never again," he said. "Never again."

She pressed her little hands against his shoulders.

"Listen! Oh, listen!"

"I shall listen to nothing."

"But you must—you must! I want to make you understand something. This morning I see your note in the papers. Every day, every day for seven whole long years, wherever I have been, I have looked. In the papers of India. Sometimes in the papers of France, of England."

"I never even dreamed that you left India," said Nicol Brinn, hoarsely. "It was through the *Times* of India that I said I would communicate with you."

"Once we never left India. Now we do—sometimes. But listen. I prepared to come when—he—"

Nicol Brinn's clasp of Naida tightened cruelly.

"Oh, you hurt me!" she moaned. "Please let me speak. He gave me your name and told me to bring you!"

"What! What!"

Nicol Brinn dropped his arms and stood, as a man amazed, watching her.

"Last night there was a meeting outside London."

"You don't want me to believe there are English members?"

"Yes. There are. Many. But let me go on. Somehow—somehow I don't understand—he finds you are one—"

"My God!"

"And you are not present last night! Now, do you understand? So he sends me to tell you that a car will be waiting at nine o'clock tonight outside the Cavalry Club. The driver will be a Hindu. You know what to say. Oh, my Nicol, my Nicol, go for my sake! You know it all! You are clever. You can pretend. You can explain you had no call. If you refuse—"

Nicol Brinn nodded grimly. "I understand! But, good God! How has he found out? How has he found out?"

87

"I don't know!" moaned Naida. "Oh, I am frightened—so frightened!"

A discreet rap sounded upon the door.

Nicol Brinn crossed and stood, hands clasped behind him, before the mantelpiece. "In," he said.

Hoskins entered. "Detective Sergeant Stokes wishes to see you at once, sir."

Brinn drew a watch from his waistcoat pocket. Attached to it was a fob from which depended a little Chinese Buddha. He consulted the timepiece and returned it to his pocket.

"Eight-twenty-five," he muttered, and glanced across to where Naida, wide-eyed, watched him. "Admit Detective Sergeant Stokes at eight-twenty. six, and then lock the door."

"Very good, sir."

Hoskins retired imperturbably.

XVI

NICOL BRINN GOES OUT

DETECTIVE SERGEANT STOKES was a big, dark, florid man, the word "constable" written all over him. Indeed, as Wessex had complained more than once, the mere sound of Stokes's footsteps was a danger signal for any crook. His respect for his immediate superior, the detective inspector, was not great. The methods of Wessex savoured too much of the French school to appeal to one of Stokes's temperament and outlook upon life, especially upon that phase of life which comes within the province of the criminal investigator.

Wessex's instructions with regard to Nicol Brinn had been succinct: "Watch Mr. Brinn's chambers, make a note of all his visitors, but take no definite steps respecting him personally without consulting me."

Armed with these instructions, the detective sergeant had undertaken his duties, which had proved more or less tedious up to the time that a fashionably attired woman of striking but unusual appearance had inquired of the hall porter upon which floor Mr. Nicol Brinn resided.

In her manner the detective sergeant had perceived something furtive. There was a hunted look in her eyes, too.

When, at the end of some fifteen or twenty minutes, she failed to reappear, he determined to take the initiative himself. By intruding upon this prolonged conference he hoped to learn something of value. Truth to tell, he was no master of finesse, and had but recently been promoted from an East End district where prompt physical action was of more value than subtlety.

As a result, then, he presently found himself in the presence of the immovable Hoskins; and having caused his name to be announced, he was requested to wait in the lobby for one minute. Exactly one minute had elapsed when he was shown into that long, lofty room, which of late had been the scene of strange happenings.

Nicol Brinn was standing before the fireplace, hands clasped behind him, and a long cigar protruding from the left corner of his mouth. No one else was present, so far as the detective could see, but he glanced rapidly about the room in a way which told the man who was watching that he had expected to find another present. He looked into the unfathomable, light blue eyes of Nicol Brinn, and became conscious of a certain mental confusion.

"Good evening, sir," he said, awkwardly. "I am acting in the case concerning the disappearance of Mr. Paul Harley."

"Yes," replied Brinn.

"I have been instructed to keep an eye on these chambers."

"Yes," repeated the high voice.

"Well, sir"—again he glanced rapidly about—"I don't want to intrude more than necessary, but a lady came in here about half an hour ago."

"Yes," drawled Brinn. "It's possible."

"It's a fact," declared the detective sergeant. "If it isn't troubling you too much, I should like to know that lady's name. Also, I should like a chat with her before she leaves."

"Can't be done," declared Nicol Brinn. "She isn't here."

"Then where is she?"

"I couldn't say. She went some time ago."

Stokes stood squarely before Nicol Brinn—a big, menacing figure; but he could not detect the slightest shadow of expression upon the other's impassive features. He began to grow angry. He was of that sanguine temperament which in anger acts hastily.

"Look here, sir," he said, and his dark face flushed. "You can't play tricks on me. I've got my duty to do, and I am going to do it. Ask your visitor to step in here, or I shall search the premises."

Nicol Brinn replaced his cigar in the right corner of his mouth: "Detective Sergeant Stokes, I give you my word that the lady to whom you refer is no longer in these chambers."

Stokes glared at him angrily. "But there is no other way out," he blustered.

"I shall not deal with this matter further," declared Brinn, coldly. "I may have vices, but I never was a liar."

"Oh," muttered the detective sergeant, taken aback by the cold incisiveness of the speaker. "Then perhaps you will lead the way, as I should like to take a look around."

Nicol Brinn spread his feet more widely upon the hearthrug. "Detective Sergeant Stokes," he said, "you are not playing the game. Inspector Wessex passed his word to me that for twenty-four hours my movements should not be questioned or interfered with. How is it that I find you here?"

Stokes thrust his hands in his pockets and coughed uneasily. "I am not a machine," he replied, "and I do my own job in my own way."

"I doubt if Inspector Wessex would approve of your way."

"That's my business."

"Maybe, but it is no affair of yours to interfere with private affairs of mine, Detective Sergeant. See here, there is no lady in these chambers. Secondly, I have an appointment at nine o'clock, and you are detaining me."

"What's more," answered Stokes, who had now quite lost his temper, "I intend to go on detaining you until I have searched these chambers and searched them thoroughly."

Nicol Brinn glanced at his watch. "If I leave in five minutes, I'll be in good time," he said. "Follow me."

Crossing to the centre section of a massive bookcase, he opened it, and it proved to be a door. So cunning was the design that the closest scrutiny must have failed to detect any difference between the dummy books with which it was decorated, and the authentic works which filled the shelves to right and to left of it. Within was a small and cosy study. In contrast with the museum-like room out of which it opened, it was furnished in a severely simple fashion, and one more experienced in the study of complex humanity than Detective Sergeant Stokes must have perceived that here the real Nicol Brinn spent his leisure hours. Above the mantel was a life-sized oil painting of Mrs. Nicolas Brinn; and whereas the great room overlooking Piccadilly was exotic to a degree, the atmosphere of the study was markedly American.

Palpably there was no one there. Nor did the two bedrooms, the kitchen, and the lobby afford any more satisfactory evidence. Nicol Brinn led the way back from the lobby, through the small study, and into the famous room where the Egyptian priestess smiled eternally. He resumed his place upon the hearthrug. "Are you satisfied, Detective Sergeant?"

"I am!" Stokes spoke angrily. "While you kept me talking, she slipped out through that study, and down into the street."

"Ah," murmured Nicol Brinn.

"In fact, the whole business looks very suspicious to me," continued the detective.

"Sorry," drawled Brinn, again consulting his watch. "The five minutes are up. I must be off."

"Not until I have spoken to Scotland Yard, sir."

"You wish to speak to Scotland Yard?"

"I do," said Stokes, grimly.

Nicol Brinn strode to the telephone, which stood upon a small table almost immediately in front of the bookcase. The masked door remained ajar.

"You are quite fixed upon detaining me?"

"Quite," said Stokes, watching him closely.

In one long stride Brinn was through the doorway, telephone in hand! Before Stokes had time to move, the door closed violently, in order, no doubt, to make it shut over the telephone cable which lay under it!

Detective Sergeant Stokes fell back, gazed wildly at the false books for a moment, and then, turning, leaped to the outer door. It was locked!

In the meanwhile, Nicol Brinn, having secured the door which communicated with the study, walked out into the lobby where Hoskins was seated. Hoskins stood up.

"The lady went, Hoskins?"

"She did, sir."

Nicol Brinn withdrew the key from the door of the room in which Detective Sergeant Stokes was confined. Stokes began banging wildly upon the panels from within.

"That row will continue," Nicol Brinn said, coldly. "Perhaps he will shout murder from one of the windows. You have only to say you had no key. I am going out now. The light coat, Hoskins."

Hoskins unemotionally handed coat, hat, and cane to his master and, opening the front door, stood aside. The sound of a window being raised became audible from within the locked room.

"Probably," added Nicol Brinn, "you will be arrested."

"Very good, sir," said Hoskins. "Good-night, sir . . ."

XVII

WHAT HAPPENED TO HARLEY

SOME TWO HOURS after Paul Harley's examination of Jones, the ex-parlourmaid, a shabby street hawker appeared in the Strand, bearing a tray containing copies of "Old Moore's Almanac." He was an ugly-looking fellow with a split lip, and appeared to have neglected to shave for at least a week. Nobody appeared to be particularly interested, and during his slow progression from Wellington Street to the Savoy Hotel he smoked cigarettes almost continuously. Trade was far from brisk, and the vendor of prophecies filled in his spare time by opening car doors, for which menial service he collected one threepenny bit and several sixpences.

This commercial optimist was still haunting the courtyard of the hotel at a time when a very handsome limousine pulled up beside the curb and a sprucely attired Hindu stepped out. One who had been in the apartments of Ormuz Khan must have recognized his excellency's private secretary. Turning to the chauffeur, a half-caste of some kind, and ignoring the presence of the prophet who had generously opened the door, "You will return at eight o'clock," he said, speaking perfect and cultured English, "to take his excellency to High Claybury. Make a note, now, as I shall be very busy, reminding me to call at Lower Claybury station for a parcel which will be awaiting me there."

"Yes, sir," replied the chauffeur, and he touched his cap as the Hindu walked into the hotel.

The salesman reclosed the door of the car, and spat reflectively upon the pavement.

Limping wearily, he worked his way along in the direction of Chancery Lane. But, before reaching Chancery Lane, he plunged into a maze of courts with which he was evidently well acquainted. His bookselling enterprise presently terminated, as it had commenced, at The Chancery Agency.

Once more safe in his dressing room, the peddler rapidly transformed himself into Paul Harley, and Paul Harley, laying his watch upon the table before him, lighted his pipe and indulged in half an hour's close thinking.

His again electing to focus his attention upon Ormuz Khan was this time beyond reproach. It was the course which logic dictated. Until he had attempted the task earlier in the day, he could not have supposed it so difficult to trace the country address of a well-known figure like that of the Persian.

This address he had determined to learn, and, having learned it, was also determined to inspect the premises. But for such a stroke of good luck as that which had befallen him at the Savoy, he could scarcely have hoped. His course now lay clearly before him. And presently, laying his pipe aside, he took up a telephone which stood upon the dressing table and rang up a garage with which he had an account.

"Hello, is that you, Mason?" he said. "Have the racer to meet me at seven o'clock, half-way along Pall Mall."

Never for a moment did he relax his vigilance. Observing every precaution when he left The Chancery Agency, he spent the intervening time at one of his clubs, from which, having made an early dinner, he set off for Pall Mall at ten minutes to seven. A rakish-looking gray car resembling a giant torpedo was approaching slowly from the direction of Buckingham Palace. The driver pulled up as Paul Harley stepped into the road, and following a brief conversation Harley set out westward, performing a detour before heading south for Lower Claybury, a little town with which he was only slightly acquainted. No evidence of espionage could he detect, but the note of danger spoke intimately to his inner consciousness; so that when, the metropolis left behind, he found himself in the hilly Surrey countryside, more than once he pulled up, sitting silent for a while and listening intently. He failed, always, to detect any sign of pursuit.

The night was tropically brilliant, hot, and still, but saving the distant murmur of the city, and ordinary comings and goings along the country roads, there was nothing to account for a growing anxiety of which he became conscious.

He was in gunshot of Old Claybury church tower, when the sight of a haystack immediately inside a meadow gate suggested a likely hiding place for the racer; and, having run the car under cover, Harley proceeded on foot to the little railway station. He approached a porter who leaned in the doorway. "Could you direct me to the house of his excellency Ormuz Khan?" he inquired.

"Yes, sir," was the reply. "If you follow the uphill road on the other side of the station until you come to the Manor Park—you will see the gates—and then branch off to the right, taking the road facing the gates. Hillside—that's the name of the house—is about a quarter of a mile along."

Dusk was beginning to fall and, although the nature of his proposed operations demanded secrecy, he recognized that every hour was precious. Accordingly he walked immediately back to the spot at which he had left the car and, following the porter's directions, drove over the line at the level crossing immediately beyond the station, and proceeded up a tree-lined road until he found himself skirting the railing of an extensive tract of park land.

Presently heavy gates appeared in view; and then, to the right, another lane in which the growing dusk had painted many shadows. He determined to drive on until he should find a suitable hiding place. And at a spot, as he presently learned, not a hundred yards from Hillside, he discovered an opening in the hedge which divided the road from a tilled field. Into this, without hesitation, he turned the racer, backing in, in order that he might be ready for a flying start in case of emergency. Once more he set out on foot.

He proceeded with caution, walking softly close to the side of the road, and frequently pausing to listen. Advancing in this fashion, he found himself standing ere long before an open gateway, and gazing along a drive which presented a vista of utter blackness. A faint sound reached his ear—the distant drone of a powerful engine. A big car was mounting the slope from Lower Claybury Station.

XVIII

HAT HAPPENED TO HARLEY—CONTINUED

NOT UNTIL HARLEY came within sight of the house, a low, rambling Jacobean building, did he attempt to take cover. He scrambled up a tree and got astride of a wall. A swift survey by his electric torch of the ground on the other side revealed a jungle of weeds in either direction.

He uttered an impatient exclamation. He calculated that the car was now within a hundred yards of the end of the lane. Suddenly came an idea that was born of emergency. Swarming up the tree to where its dense foliage began, he perched upon a stout bough and waited.

Three minutes later came a blaze of light through the gathering darkness, and the car which he had last seen at the Savoy was turned into the drive, and presently glided smoothly past him below.

The interior lights were extinguished, so that he was unable to discern the occupants. The house itself was also unilluminated. And when the car pulled up before the porch, less than ten yards from his observation post, he could not have recognized the persons who descended and entered Hillside.

Indeed, only by the sound of the closing door did he know that they had gone in. But two figures were easily discernible; and he judged them to be those of Ormuz Khan and his secretary. He waited patiently, and ere long the limousine was turned in the little courtyard before the porch and driven out into the lane again. He did not fail to note that, the lane regained, the chauffeur headed, not toward Lower Claybury, but away from it.

He retained his position until the hum of the motor grew dim in the distance, and was about to descend when he detected the sound of a second approaching car! Acutely conscious of danger, he remained where he was. Almost before the hum of the retiring limousine had become inaudible, a second car entered the lane and turned into the drive of Hillside.

Harley peered eagerly downward, half closing his eyes in order that he might not be dazzled by the blaze of the headlight. This was another limousine, its most notable characteristic being that the blinds were drawn in all the windows.

On this occasion, when the chauffeur stepped around and opened the door, only one passenger alighted. There seemed to be some delay before he was admitted, but Harley found it impossible to detect any details of the scene being enacted in the shadowed porch.

Presently the second car was driven away, pursuing the same direction as the first. Hot upon its departure came the drone of a third.

The windows of the third car also exhibited drawn blinds. As it passed beneath him he stifled an exclamation of triumph. Vaguely, nebulously, the secret of this dread thing Fire-Tongue, which had uplifted its head in England, appeared before his mind's eye. It was only necessary for him to assure himself that the latest visitor had been admitted to the house before the next move became possible. Accordingly he changed his position, settling himself more comfortably upon the bough. And now he watched the three cars perform each two journeys to some spot or spots unknown, and, returning, deposit their passengers before the porch of Hillside. The limousine used by Ormuz Khan, upon its second appearance had partaken of the same peculiarity as the others: there were blinds drawn inside the windows.

Paul Harley believed that he understood precisely what this signified, and when, after listening intently in the stillness of the night, he failed to detect sounds of any other approach, he descended to the path and stole toward the dark house.

There were French windows upon the ground floor, all of them closely shuttered. Although he recognized that he was taking desperate chances, he inspected each one of them closely.

Passing gently from window to window, his quest ultimately earned its reward. Through a crack in one of the shutters a dim light shone out. His heart was beating uncomfortably, although he had himself well in hand; and, crawling into the recess formed by the window, he pressed his ear against a pane and listened intently. At first he could hear nothing, but, his investigation being aided by the stillness of the night, he presently became aware that a voice was speaking within the room—deliberately, musically. The beating of his heart seemed to make his body throb to the very finger tips. He had recognized the voice to be the voice of Ormuz Khan!

Now, his sense of hearing becoming attuned to the muffled tones, he began to make out syllables, words, and, finally, sentences. Darkness wrapped him about, so that no one watching could have seen his face. But he himself knew that under the bronze which he never lost he had grown pale. His heartbeats grew suddenly fainter, an eerie chill more intense than any which the note of danger had ever occasioned caused him to draw sharply back.

"My God!" he whispered. He drew his automatic swiftly from his pocket, and, pressed against the wall beside the window, looked about him as a man looks who finds himself surrounded by enemies. Not a sound disturbed the stillness of the garden except for sibilant rustlings of the leaves, occasioned by a slight breeze.

Paul Harley retreated step by step to the bushes. He held the pistol tightly clenched in his right hand.

He had heard his own death sentence pronounced and he knew that it was likely to be executed.

XIX

WHAT HAPPENED TO HARLEY—CONCLUDED

HE REGAINED THE curve of the drive without meeting any opposition. There, slipping the pistol into his pocket, he climbed rapidly up the tree from which he had watched the arrival of the three cars, climbed over the wall, and dropped into the weed jungle beyond. He crept stealthily forward to the gap where he had concealed the racer, drawing nearer and nearer to the bushes lining the lane. Only by a patch of greater darkness before him did he realize that he had reached it. But when the realization came one word only he uttered: "Gone!"

His car had disappeared!

Despair was alien to his character: A true Englishman, he never knew when he was beaten. Beyond doubt, now, he must accept the presence of hidden enemies surrounding him, of enemies whose presence even his trained powers of perception had been unable to detect. The intensity of the note of danger which he had recognized now was fully explained. He grew icily cool, master of his every faculty. "We shall see!" he muttered, grimly.

Feeling his way into the lane, he set out running for the highroad, his footsteps ringing out sharply upon the dusty way. The highroad gained, he turned, not to the left, but to the right, ran up the bank and threw himself flatly down upon it, lying close to the hedge and watching the entrance to the lane. Nothing appeared; nothing stirred. He knew the silence to be illusive; he blamed himself for having ventured upon such a quest without acquainting himself with the geography of the neighbourhood.

Great issues often rest upon a needle point. He had no idea of the direction or extent of the park land adjoining the highroad. Nevertheless, further inaction being out of the question, creeping along the grassy bank, he began to retreat from the entrance to the lane. Some ten yards he had progressed in this fashion when his hidden watchers made their first mistake.

A faint sound, so faint that only a man in deadly peril could have detected it, brought him up sharply. He crouched back against the hedge, looking behind him. For a long time he failed to observe anything. Then, against the comparatively high tone of the dusty road, he saw a silhouette—the head and shoulders of someone who peered out cautiously.

Still as the trees above him he crouched, watching, and presently, bent forward, questing to right and left, questing in a horribly suggestive animal fashion, the entire figure of the man appeared in the roadway.

As Paul Harley had prayed would be the case, his pursuers evidently believed that he had turned in the direction of Lower Claybury. A vague, phantom figure, Harley saw the man wave his arm, whereupon a second man joined him—a third—and, finally, a fourth.

Harley clenched his teeth grimly, and as the ominous quartet began to move toward the left, he resumed his slow retreat to the right— going ever farther away, of necessity, from the only centre with which he was acquainted and from which he could hope to summon assistance. Finally he reached a milestone resting almost against the railings of the Manor Park.

Drawing a deep breath, he sprang upon the milestone, succeeded in grasping the top of the high iron railings, and hauled himself up bodily.

Praying that the turf might be soft, he jumped. Fit though he was, and hardened by physical exercise, the impact almost stunned him. He came down like an acrobat—left foot, right foot, and then upon his hands, but nevertheless he lay there for a moment breathless and temporarily numbed by the shock.

In less than a minute he was on his feet again and looking alertly about him. Striking into the park land, turning to the left, and paralleling the highroad, he presently came out upon the roadway, along which under shelter of a straggling hedge, he began to double back. In sight of the road dipping down to Lower Claybury he crossed, forcing his way through a second hedge thickly sown with thorns.

Badly torn, but careless of such minor injuries, he plunged heavily through a turnip field, and, bearing always to the left, came out finally upon the road leading to the station, and only some fifty yards from the bottom of the declivity.

A moment he paused, questioning the silence. He was unwilling to believe that he had outwitted his pursuers. His nerves were strung to highest tension, and his strange gift of semi- prescience told him that danger was at least as imminent as ever, even though he could neither see nor hear his enemies. Therefore, pistol in hand again, he descended to the foot of the hill.

He remembered having noticed, when he had applied to the porter for information respecting the residence of Ormuz Khan, that upon a window adjoining the entrance had appeared the words "Station Master." The station master's office, therefore, was upon the distant side of the line.

Now came the hardest blow of all. The station was closed for the night. Nor was there any light in the signal box. Evidently no other train was due upon that branch line until some time in the early morning. The level crossing gate was open, but before breaking cover he paused a while to consider what he should do. Lower Claybury was one of those stations which have no intimate connection with any township. The nearest house, so far as Harley could recall, was fully twenty yards from the spot at which he stood. Furthermore, the urgency of the case had fired the soul of the professional investigator.

He made up his mind, and, darting out into the road, he ran across the line, turned sharply, and did not pause until he stood before the station master's window. Then his quick wits were put to their ultimate test.

Right, left, it seemed from all about him, came swiftly pattering footsteps! Instantly he divined the truth. Losing his tracks upon the highroad above, a section of his pursuers had surrounded the station, believing that he would head for it in retreat.

Paul Harley whipped off his coat in a flash, and using it as a ram, smashed the window. He reached up, found the catch, and opened the sash. In ten seconds he was in the room, and a great clatter told him that he had overturned some piece of furniture.

Disentangling his coat, he sought and found the electric torch. He pressed the button. No light came. It was broken! He drew a hissing breath, and began to grope about the little room. At last his hand touched the telephone, and, taking it up:

"Hello!" he said. "Hello!"

"Yes," came the voice of the operator—"what number?"

"City 8951. Police business! Urgent!"

One, two, three seconds elapsed, four, five, six.

"Hello!" came the voice of Innes.

"That you, Innes?" said Harley. And, interrupting the other's reply: "I am by no means safe, Innes! I am in one of the tightest corners of my life. Listen: Get Wessex! If he's off duty, get Burton. Tell him to bring—"

Someone leaped in at the broken window behind the speaker. Resting the telephone upon the table, where he had found it, Harley reached into his hip pocket and snapped out his automatic.

Dimly he could hear Innes speaking. He half-turned, raised the pistol, and knew a sudden intense pain at the back of his skull. A thousand lights seemed suddenly to split the darkness. He felt himself sinking into an apparently bottomless pit.

XX

CONFLICTING CLUBS

"ANY NEWS, Wessex?" asked Innes, eagerly, starting up from his chair as the inspector entered the office.

Wessex shook his head, and sitting down took out and lighted a cigarette.

"News of a sort," he replied, slowly, "but nothing of any value, I am afraid. My assistant, Stokes, has distinguished himself."

"In what way?" asked Innes, dully, dropping back into his chair.

These were trying days for the indefatigable secretary. Believing that some clue of importance might come to light at any hour of the day or night he remained at the chambers in Chancery Lane, sleeping nightly in the spare room.

"Well," continued the inspector, "I had detailed him to watch Nicol Brinn, but my explicit instructions were that Nicol Brinn was not to be molested in any way."

"What happened?"

"Tonight Nicol Brinn had a visitor—possibly a valuable witness. Stokes, like an idiot, allowed her to slip through his fingers and tried to arrest Brinn!"

"What? Arrest him!" cried Innes.

"Precisely. But I rather fancy," added the inspector, grimly, "that Mr. Stokes will think twice before taking leaps like that in the dark again."

"You say he tried to arrest him. What do you mean by that?"

"I mean that Nicol Brinn, leaving Stokes locked in his chambers, went out and has completely disappeared!"

"But the woman?"

"Ah, the woman! There's the rub. If he had lain low and followed the woman, all might have been well. But who she was, where she came from, and where she has gone, we have no idea."

"Nicol Brinn must have been desperate to adopt such measures?"

Detective Inspector Wessex nodded.

"I quite agree with you."

"He evidently had an appointment of such urgency that he could permit nothing to stand in his way."

"He is a very clever man, Mr. Innes. He removed the telephone from the room in which he had locked Stokes, so that my blundering assistant was detained for nearly fifteen minutes—detained, in fact, until his cries from the window attracted the attention of a passing constable!"

"Nicol Brinn's man did not release him?"

"No, he said he had no key."

"What happened?"

"Stokes wanted to detain the servant, whose name is Hoskins, but I simply wouldn't hear of it. I am a poor man, but I would cheerfully give fifty pounds to know where Nicol Brinn is at this moment."

Innes stood up restlessly and began to drum his fingers upon the table edge. Presently he looked up, and:

"There's a shadow of hope," he said. "Rector—you know Rector?—had been detailed by the chief to cover the activities of Nicol Brinn. He has not reported to me so far tonight."

"You mean that he may be following him?" cried Wessex.

"It is quite possible—following either Nicol Brinn or the woman."

"My God, I hope you're right!—even though it makes the Criminal Investigation Department look a bit silly."

"Then," continued Innes, "there is something else which you should know. I heard today from a garage, with which Mr. Harley does business, that he hired a racing car last night. He has often used it before. It met him half-way along Pall Mall at seven o'clock, and he drove away in it in the direction of Trafalgar Square."

"Alone?"

"Yes, unfortunately."

"Toward Trafalgar Square," murmured Wessex.

"Ah," said Innes, shaking his head, "that clue is of no importance. Under the circumstances the chief would be much more likely to head away from his objective than toward it."

"Quite," murmured Wessex. "I agree with you. But what's this?"

The telephone bell was ringing, and as Innes eagerly took up the receiver:

"Yes, yes, Mr. Innes speaking," he said, quickly. "Is that you, Rector?"

The voice of Rector, one of Paul Harley's assistants, answered him over the wire:

"I am speaking from Victoria Station, Mr. Innes."

"Yes!" said Innes. "Go ahead."

"A very odd-looking woman visited Mr. Nicol Brinn's chambers this evening. She was beautifully dressed, but wore the collar of her fur coat turned up about her face, so that it was difficult to see her. But somehow I think she was an Oriental."

"An Oriental!" exclaimed Innes.

"I waited for her to come out," Rector continued. "She had arrived in a cab, which was waiting, and I learned from the man that he had picked her up at Victoria Station."

"Yes?"

"She came out some time later in rather a hurry. In fact, I think there was no doubt that she was frightened. By this time I had another cab waiting."

"And where did she go?" asked Innes.

"Back to Victoria Station."

"Yes! Go on!"

"Unfortunately, Mr. Innes, my story does not go much further. I wasted very little time, you may be sure. But although no train had left from the South Eastern station, which she had entered, there was no sign of her anywhere. So that I can only suppose she ran through to the Brighton side, or possibly out to a car, which may have been waiting for her somewhere."

"Is that all?" asked Innes, gloomily.

"That's all, Mr. Innes. But I thought I would report it."

"Quite right, Rector; you could do no more. Did you see anything of Detective Sergeant Stokes before you left Piccadilly?"

"I did," replied the other. "He also was intensely interested in Nicol Brinn's visitor. And about five minutes before she came out he went upstairs."

"Oh, I see. She came out almost immediately after Stokes had gone up?"

"Yes."

"Very well, Rector. Return to Piccadilly, and report to me as soon as possible." Innes hung up the receiver.

"Did you follow, Wessex?" he said. "Stokes was on the right track, but made a bad blunder. You see, his appearance led to the woman's retreat."

"He explained that to me," returned the inspector, gloomily. "She got out by another door as he came in. Oh! a pretty mess he has made of it. If he and Rector had been cooperating, they could have covered her movements perfectly."

"There is no use crying over spilt milk," returned Innes. He glanced significantly in the inspector's direction. "Miss Abingdon has rung up practically every hour all day," he said.

Wessex nodded his head.

"I'm a married man myself," he replied, "and happily married, too. But if you had seen the look in her eyes when I told her that Mr. Harley had disappeared, I believe you would have envied him."

"Yes," murmured Innes. "They haven't known each other long, but I should say from what little I have seen of them that she cares too much for her peace of mind." He stared hard at the inspector. "I think it will break her heart if anything has happened to the chief. The sound of her voice over the telephone brings a lump into my throat, Wessex. She rang up an hour ago. She will ring up again."

"Yet I never thought he was a marrying man," muttered the inspector.

"Neither did I," returned Innes, smiling sadly. "But even he can be forgiven for changing his mind in the case of Phil Abingdon."

"Ah," said the inspector. "I am not sorry to know that he is human like the rest of us." His expression grew retrospective, and: "I can't make out how the garage you were speaking about didn't report that matter before," he added.

"Well, you see," explained Innes, "they were used to the chief making long journeys."

"Long journeys," muttered the inspector. "Did he make a long journey? I wonder—I wonder."

XXI

THE SEVENTH KAMA

AS NICOL BRINN strolled out from the door below his chambers in Piccadilly, a hoarse voice made itself audible above his head.

"Police!" he heard over the roar of the traffic. "Help! Police!"

Detective Sergeant Stokes had come out upon the balcony. But up to the time that Nicol Brinn turned and proceeded in leisurely fashion in the direction of the Cavalry Club, the sergeant had not succeeded in attracting any attention.

Nicol Brinn did not hurry. Having his hands thrust in the pockets of his light overcoat, he sauntered along Piccadilly as an idle man might do. He knew that he had ample time to keep his appointment, and recognizing the vital urgency of the situation, he was grateful for some little leisure to reject.

One who had obtained a glimpse of his face in the light of the shop windows which he passed must have failed to discern any evidence of anxiety. Yet Nicol Brinn knew that death was beckoning to him. He knew that his keen wit was the only weapon which could avail him tonight; and he knew that he must show himself a master of fence.

A lonely man, of few but enduring friendships, he had admitted but one love to his life, except the love of his mother. This one love for seven years he had sought to kill. But anything forceful enough to penetrate to the stronghold of Nicol Brinn's soul was indestructible, even by Nicol Brinn himself.

So, now, at the end of a mighty struggle, he had philosophically accepted this hopeless passion which Fate had thrust upon him. Yet he whose world was a chaos outwardly remained unmoved.

Perhaps even that evil presence whose name was Fire-Tongue might have paused, might have hesitated, might even have changed his plans, which, in a certain part of the world, were counted immutable, had he known the manner of man whom he had summoned to him that night.

Just outside the Cavalry Club a limousine was waiting, driven by a chauffeur who looked like some kind of Oriental. Nicol Brinn walked up to the man, and bending forward:

"Fire-Tongue," he said, in a low voice.

The chauffeur immediately descended and opened the door of the car. The interior was unlighted, but Nicol Brinn cast a comprehensive glance around ere entering. As he settled himself upon the cushions, the door was closed again, and he found himself in absolute darkness.

"Ah," he muttered. "Might have foreseen it." All the windows were curtained, or rather, as a rough investigation revealed, were closed with aluminum shutters which were immovable.

A moment later, as the car moved off, a lamp became lighted above him. Then he saw that several current periodicals were placed invitingly in the rack, as well as a box of very choice Egyptian cigarettes.

"H'm," he murmured.

He made a close investigation upon every side, but he knew enough of the organization with which he was dealing to be prepared for failure.

He failed. There was no cranny through which he could look out. Palpably, it would be impossible to learn where he was being taken. The journey might be a direct one, or might be a detour. He wished that he could have foreseen this device. Above all, he wished that Detective Sergeant Stokes had been a more clever man.

It would have been good to know that he was followed. His only hope was that someone detailed by Paul Harley might be in pursuit.

Lighting a fresh cigar, Nicol Brinn drew a copy of the Sketch from the rack, and studied the photographs of more or less pretty actresses with apparent contentment. He had finished the Sketch, and was perusing the Bystander, when, the car having climbed a steep hill and swerved sharply to the right, he heard the rustling of leaves, and divined that they were proceeding along a drive.

He replaced the paper in the rack, and took out his watch. Consulting it, he returned it to his pocket as the car stopped and the light went out.

The door, which, with its fellow, Nicol Brinn had discovered to be locked, was opened by the Oriental chauffeur, and Brinn descended upon the steps of a shadowed porch. The house door was open, and although there was no light within:

"Come this way," said a voice, speaking out of the darkness.

Nicol Brinn entered a hallway the atmosphere of which seemed to be very hot.

"Allow me to take your hat and coat," continued the voice.

He was relieved of these, guided along a dark passage; and presently, an inner door being opened, he found himself in a small, barely furnished room where one shaded lamp burned upon a large writing table.

His conductor, who did not enter, closed the door quietly, and Nicol Brinn found himself looking into the smiling face of a Hindu gentleman who sat at the table.

The room was decorated with queer-looking Indian carvings, pictures upon silk, and other products of Eastern craftsmanship. The table and the several chairs were Oriental in character, but the articles upon the table were very European and businesslike in appearance. Furthermore, the Hindu gentleman, who wore correct evening dress, might have been the representative of an Eastern banking house, as indeed he happened to be, amongst other things.

"Good evening," he said, speaking perfect English "won't you sit down?"

He pointed with a pen which he was holding in the direction of a heavily carved chair which stood near the table. Nicol Brinn sat down, regarding the speaker with lack-lustre eyes.

"A query has arisen respecting your fraternal rights," continued the Hindu. "Am I to understand that you claim to belong to the Seventh Kama?"

"Certainly," replied Brinn in a toneless voice.

The Hindu drew his cuff back from a slender yellow wrist, revealing a curious mark which appeared to be branded upon the flesh. It was in the form of a torch or flambeau surmounted by a tongue of flame. He raised his black brows, smiling significantly.

Nicol Brinn stood up, removing his tight dinner jacket. Then, rolling back his sleeve from a lean, sinuous forearm, he extended the powerful member, having his fist tightly clenched.

Upon the inside of his arm, just above the elbow, an identical mark had been branded!

The Hindu stood up and saluted Nicol Brinn in a peculiar manner. That is to say, he touched the second finger of his right hand with the tip of his tongue, and then laid the finger upon his forehead, at the same time bowing deeply.

Nicol Brinn repeated the salutation, and quietly put his coat on.

"We greet you," said the Hindu. "I am Rama Dass of the Bengal Lodge. Have you Hindustani?"

"No."

"Where were you initiated?"

"At Moon Ali Lane."

"Ah!" exclaimed the Hindu. "I see it all. In Bombay?"

"In Bombay."

"When, and by whom, may I ask?"

"By Ruhmani, November 23, 1913."

"Strange," murmured Rama Dass. "Brother Ruhmani died in that year; which accounts for our having lost touch with you. What is your grade?"

"The fifth."

"You have not proceeded far, brother. How do you come to be unacquainted with our presence in England?"

"I cannot say."

"What work has been allotted to you?"

"None."

"Never?"

"Never."

"More and more strange," murmured the Hindu, watching Nicol

Brinn through the gold-rimmed spectacles which he wore. "I have only known one other case. Such cases are dangerous, brother."

"No blame attaches to me," replied Nicol Brinn.

"I have not said so," returned Rama Dass. "But in the Seventh Kama all brothers must work. A thousand lives are as nothing so the Fire lives. We had thought our information perfect, but only by accident did we learn of your existence."

"Indeed," murmured Nicol Brinn, coldly.

Not even this smiling Hindu gentleman, whose smile concealed so much, could read any meaning in those lack-lustre eyes, nor detect any emotion in that high, cool voice.

"A document was found, and in this it was recorded that you bore upon your arm the sign of the Seventh Kama."

"'Tis Fire that moves the grains of dust," murmured Nicol Brinn, tonelessly, "which one day make a mountain for the gods."

Rama Dass stood up at once and repeated his strange gesture of salutation, which Nicol Brinn returned ceremoniously; and resumed his seat at the table.

"You are advanced beyond your grade, brother," he said. "You are worthy the next step. Do you wish to take it?"

"Every little drop swells the ocean," returned Nicol Brinn.

"You speak well," the Hindu said. "We have here your complete record. It shall not be consulted. To do so were unnecessary. We are satisfied. We regret only that one so happily circumstanced to promote the coming of the Fire should have been lost sight of. Last night there were three promotions and several rejections. You were expected."

"But I was not summoned."

"No," murmured Rama Dass. "We had learned of you as I have said. However, great honour results. You will be received alone. Do you desire to advance?"

"No. Give me time."

Rama Dass again performed the strange salutation, and again Nicol Brinn returned it.

"Wisdom is a potent wine," said the latter, gravely.

"We respect your decision."

The Hindu rang a little silver bell upon his table, and the double doors which occupied one end of the small room opened silently, revealing a large shadowy apartment beyond.

Rama Dass stood up, crossed the room, and standing just outside the open doors, beckoned to Nicol Brinn to advance.

"There is no fear," he said, in a queer, chanting tone.

"There is no fear," repeated Nicol Brinn.

"There is no love."

"There is no love."

"There is no death."

"There is no death."

"Fire alone is eternal."

"Fire alone is eternal."

As he pronounced those words Nicol Brinn crossed the threshold of the dark room, and the double doors closed silently behind him.

XXII

FIRE-TONGUE SPEAKS

ABSOLUTE DARKNESS SURROUNDED Nicol Brinn. Darkness, unpleasant heat, and a stifling odour of hyacinths. He had been well coached, and thus far his memory had served him admirably. But now he knew not what to expect. Therefore inwardly on fire but outwardly composed, muscles taut and nerves strung highly, he waited for the next development.

It took the form, first, of the tinkling of a silver bell, and then of the coming of a dim light at the end of what was evidently a long apartment. The light grew brighter, assuming the form of a bluish flame burning in a little flambeau. Nicol Brinn watched it fascinatedly.

Absolutely no sound was discernible, until a voice began to speak, a musical voice of curiously arresting quality.

"You are welcome," said the voice. "You are of the Bombay Lodge, although a citizen of the United States. Because of some strange error, no work has been allotted to you hitherto. This shall be remedied."

Of the weird impressiveness of the scene there could be no doubt. It even touched some unfamiliar chord in the soul of Nicol Brinn. The effect of such an interview upon an imaginative, highly strung temperament, could be well imagined. It was perhaps theatrical, but that by such means great ends had already been achieved he knew to his cost.

The introduction of Maskelyne illusions into an English country house must ordinarily have touched his sense of humour, but knowing something of the invisible presence in which he stood in that darkened chamber, there was no laughter in the heart of Nicol Brinn, but rather an unfamiliar coldness, the nearest approach to fear of which this steel-nerved man was capable.

"Temporarily," the sweet voice continued, "you will be affiliated with the London Lodge, to whom you will look for instructions. These will reach you almost immediately. There is great work to be done in England. It has been decided, however, that you shall be transferred as quickly as possible in our New York Lodge. You will await orders. Only Fire is eternal."

Again the voice ceased. But, Nicol Brinn remained silent:

"Your reply is awaited."

"Fire is life," replied Nicol Brinn.

The blue tongue of flame subsided, lower and lower, and finally disappeared, so that the apartment became enwrapped in absolute darkness. A faint rustling sound suggested that a heavy curtain had been lowered, and almost immediately the doors behind Nicol Brinn were opened again by Rama Dass.

"We congratulate you, brother," he said, extending his hand. "Yet the ordeal was no light one, for all the force of the Fire was focused upon you."

Nicol Brinn reentered the room where the shaded lamp stood upon the writing table. In the past he had moved unscathed through peril unknown to the ordinary man. He was well acquainted with the resources of the organization whose agents, unseen, surrounded him in that remote country house, but that their pretensions were extravagant his present immunity would seem to prove.

If the speaker with the strangely arresting voice were indeed that Fire-Tongue whose mere name was synonymous with dread in certain parts of the East, then Fire-Tongue was an impostor. He who claimed to read the thoughts of all men had signally failed in the present instance, unless Nicol Brinn stared dully into the smiling face of Rama Dass. Not yet must he congratulate himself. Perhaps the Hindu's smile concealed as much as the mask worn by Nicol Brinn.

"We congratulate you," said Rama Dass. "You are a worthy brother."

He performed the secret salutation, which Nicol Brinn automatically acknowledged. Then, without another word, Rama Dass led the way to the door.

Out into the dark hallway Nicol Brinn stepped, his muscles taut, his brain alert for instant action. But no one offered to molest him. He was assisted into his coat, and his hat was placed in his hands. Then, the front door being opened, he saw the headlights of the waiting car shining on a pillar of the porch.

A minute later he was seated again in the shuttered limousine, and as it moved off, and the lights leapt up above him, he lay back upon the cushions and uttered a long sigh.

Already he divined that, following a night's sleep, these scenes would seem like the episodes of a dream. Taking off his hat, he raised his hand to his forehead, and discovered it to be slightly damp.

"No wonder," he muttered.

Drawing out a silk handkerchief from the breast pocket of his dinner jacket, he wiped his face and forehead deliberately. Then, selecting a long black cigar from a case which bore the monogram of the late Czar of Russia, he lighted it, dropped the match in the tray, and lolling back in a corner, closed his eyes wearily.

Thus, almost unmoving, he remained throughout the drive. His only actions were, first, to assure himself that both doors were locked again, and then at intervals tidily to place a little cone of ash in the tray provided for the purpose. Finally, the car drew up and a door was unlocked by the chauffeur.

Nicol Brinn, placing his hat upon his head, stepped out before the porch of the Cavalry Club.

The chauffeur closed the door, and returned again to the wheel. Immediately the car moved away. At the illuminated number Nicol Brinn scarcely troubled to glance. Common sense told him that it was not that under which the car was registered. His interest, on the contrary, was entirely focused upon a beautiful Rolls Royce, which was evidently awaiting some visitor or member of the club. Glancing shrewdly at the chauffeur, a smart, military-looking fellow, Nicol Brinn drew a card from his waistcoat pocket, and resting it upon a wing in the light of one of the lamps, wrote something rapidly upon it in pencil.

Returning the pencil to his pocket:

"Whose car, my man?" he inquired of the chauffeur.

"Colonel Lord Wolverham's, sir."

"Good," said Nicol Brinn, and put the card and a ten-shilling note into the man's hand. "Go right into the club and personally give Colonel Lord Wolverham this card. Do you understand?"

The man understood. Used to discipline, he recognized the note of command in the speaker's voice.

"Certainly, sir," he returned, without hesitation; and stepping down upon the pavement he walked into the club.

Less than two minutes afterward a highly infuriated military gentleman—who, as it chanced, had never even heard of the distinguished American traveller—came running out hatless into Piccadilly, holding a crumpled visiting card in his hand. The card, which his chauffeur had given him in the midst of a thrilling game, read as follows:

MR. NICOL BRINN
RALEIGH HOUSE, PICCADILLY, W. I.

And written in pencil beneath the name appeared the following:

Borrowed your Rolls. Urgent.
Will explain tomorrow. Apologize.
N.B.

XXIII

PHIL ABINGDON'S VISITOR

ON THE FOLLOWING morning the card of His Excellency Ormuz Khan was brought to Phil Abingdon in the charming little room which Mrs. McMurdoch had allotted to her for a private sanctum during the period of her stay under this hospitable roof.

"Oh," she exclaimed, and looked at the maid in a startled way. "I suppose I must see him. Will you ask him to come in, please?"

A few moments later Ormuz Khan entered. He wore faultless morning dress, too faultless; so devoid of any flaw or crease as to have lost its masculine character. In his buttonhole was a hyacinth, and in one slender ivory hand he carried a huge bunch of pink roses, which, bowing deeply, he presented to the embarrassed girl.

"Dare I venture," he said in his musical voice, bending deeply over her extended hand, "to ask you to accept these flowers? It would honour me. Pray do not refuse."

"Your excellency is very kind," she replied, painfully conscious of acute nervousness. "It is more than good of you."

"It is good of you to grant me so much pleasure," he returned, sinking gracefully upon a settee, as Phil Abingdon resumed her seat. "Condolences are meaningless. Why should I offer them to one of your acute perceptions? But you know"—the long, magnetic eyes regarded her fixedly—"you know what is in my heart."

Phil Abingdon bit her lip, merely nodding in reply.

"Let us then try to forget, if only for a while," said Ormuz Khan. "I could show you so easily, if you would consent to allow me, that those we love never leave us."

The spell of his haunting voice was beginning to have its effect. Phil Abingdon found herself fighting against something which at once repelled and attracted her. She had experienced this unusual attraction before, and this was not the first time that she had combated it. But whereas formerly she had more or less resigned herself to the strange magic which lay in the voice and in the eyes of Ormuz Khan, this morning there was something within her which rebelled fiercely against the Oriental seductiveness of his manner.

She recognized that a hot flush had covered her cheeks. For the image of Paul Harley, bronzed, gray-eyed, and reproachful, had appeared before her mind's eye, and she knew why her resentment of the Persian's charm of manner had grown so intense. Yet she was not wholly immune from it, for:

"Does Your Excellency really mean that?" she whispered.

A smile appeared upon his face, an alluring smile, but rather that of a beautiful woman than of a man.

"As you of the West," he said, "have advanced step by step, ever upward in the mechanical sciences, we of the East have advanced also step by step in other and greater sciences."

"Certainly," she admitted, "you have spoken of such things before."

"I speak of things which I know. From that hour when you entered upon your first Kama, back in the dawn of time, until now, those within the ever-moving cycle which bears you on through the ages have been beside you, at times unseen by the world, at times unseen by you, veiled by the mist which men call death, but which is no more than a curtain behind which we sometimes step for a while. In the East we have learned to raise that curtain; in the West are triflers who make like claims, but whose knowledge of the secret of the veil is—" And he snapped his fingers contemptuously.

The strange personality of the man was having its effect. Phil Abingdon's eyes were widely open, and she was hanging upon his words. Underneath the soft effeminate exterior lay a masterful spirit— a spirit which had known few obstacles. The world of womanhood could have produced no more difficult subject than Phil Abingdon. Yet she realized, and became conscious of a sense of helplessness, that under certain conditions she would be as a child in the hands of this Persian mystic, whose weird eyes appeared to be watching not her body, nor even her mind, but her soul, whose voice touched unfamiliar chords within her—chords which had never responded to any other human voice.

It was thrilling, vaguely pleasurable, but deep terror underlay it.

"Your Excellency almost frightens me," she whispered. "Yet I do not doubt that you speak of what you know."

"It is so," he returned, gravely. "At any hour, day or night, if you care to make the request, I shall be happy to prove my words. But," he lowered his dark lashes and then raised them again, "the real object of my visit is concerned with more material things."

"Indeed," said Phil Abingdon, and whether because of the words of Ormuz Khan, or because of some bond of telepathy which he had established between them, she immediately found herself to be thinking of Paul Harley.

"I bring you a message," he continued, "from a friend."

With eyes widely open, Phil Abingdon watched him.

"From," she began—but her lips would not frame the name.

"From Mr. Paul Harley," he said, inclining his head gravely.

"Oh! tell me, tell me!"

"I am here to tell you, Miss Abingdon. Mr. Harley feels that his absence may have distressed you."

"Yes, yes," she said, eagerly.

"But in pursuit of a certain matter which is known to you, he has found it necessary in the interests of his safety to remain out of London for a while."

"Oh," Phil Abingdon heaved a great sigh. "Oh, Your Excellency, how glad I am to hear that he is safe!"

The long, dark eyes regarded her intently, unemotionally, noting that the flush had faded from her face, leaving it very pale, and noting also the expression of gladness in her eyes, the quivering of her sweet lips.

"He is my guest," continued Ormuz Khan, "my honoured guest."

"He is with you?" exclaimed Phil, almost incredulously.

"With me, at my home in Surrey. In me he found a natural ally, since my concern was as great as his own. I do not conceal from you, Miss Abingdon, that he is danger."

"In danger?" she whispered.

"It is true, but beneath my roof he is safe. There is a matter of vital urgency, however, in which you can assist him."

"I?" she exclaimed.

"No one but you." Ormuz Khan raised his slender hand gracefully. "I beg you, do not misunderstand me. In the first place, would Mr. Harley have asked you to visit him at my home, if he had not been well assured that you could do so with propriety? In the second place, should I, who respect you more deeply than any woman in the world, consent to your coming unchaperoned? Miss Abingdon, you know me better. I beg of you in Mr. Harley's name and in my own, prevail upon Mrs. McMurdoch to accept the invitation which I bring to lunch with me at Hillside, my Surrey home."

He spoke with the deep respect of a courtier addressing his queen. His low musical voice held a note that was almost a note of adoration. Phil Abingdon withdrew her gaze from the handsome ivory face, and strove for mental composure before replying.

Subtly, insidiously, the man had cast his spell upon her. Of this she was well aware. In other words, her thoughts were not entirely her own, but in a measure were promptings from that powerful will.

Indeed, her heart was beating wildly at the mere thought that she was to see Paul Harley again that very day. She had counted the hours since their last meeting, and knew exactly how many had elapsed. Because each one had seemed like twelve, she had ceased to rebel against this sweet weakness, which, for the first time in her life, had robbed her of some of her individuality, and had taught her that she was a woman to whom mastery by man is exquisite slavery. Suddenly she spoke.

"Of course I will come, Your Excellency," she said. "I will see Mrs. McMurdoch at once, but I know she will not refuse."

"Naturally she will not refuse, Miss Abingdon," he returned In a grave voice. "The happiness of so many people is involved."

"It is so good of you," she said, standing up. "I shall never forget your kindness."

He rose, bowing deeply, from a European standpoint too deeply.

"Kindness is a spiritual investment," he said, "which returns us interest tenfold. If I can be sure of Mrs. McMurdoch's acceptance, I will request permission to take my leave now, for I have an urgent business appointment to keep, after which I will call for you. Can you be ready by noon?"

"Yes, we shall be ready."

Phil Abingdon held out her hand in a curiously hesitant manner. The image of Paul Harley had become more real, more insistent. Her mind was in a strangely chaotic state, so that when the hand of Ormuz Khan touched her own, she repressed a start and laughed in an embarrassed way.

She knew that her heart was singing, but under the song lay something cold, and when Ormuz Khan had bowed himself from the room, she found herself thinking, not of the newly departed visitor, nor even of Paul Harley, but of her dead father. In spite of the sunshine which flooded the room, her flesh turned cold and she wondered if the uncanny Persian possessed some strange power.

Clearly as though he had stood beside her, she seemed to hear the beloved voice of her father. It was imagination, of course, she knew this; but it was uncannily real.

She thought that he was calling her, urgently, beseechingly:

"Phil . . . Phil . . ."

XXIV

THE SCREEN OF GOLD

PAUL HARLEY RAISED his aching head and looked wearily about him. At first, as might be expected, he thought that he was dreaming. He lay upon a low divan and could only suppose that he had been transported to India.

Slowly, painfully, memory reasserted itself and he realized that he had been rendered unconscious by the blow of a sandbag or some similar weapon while telephoning from the station master's office at Lower Claybury. How long a time had elapsed since that moment he was unable to judge, for his watch had been removed from his pocket. He stared about him with a sort of fearful interest. He lay in a small barely furnished room having white distempered walls, wholly undecorated. Its few appointments were Oriental, and the only window which it boasted was set so high as to be well out of reach. Moreover, it was iron-barred, and at the moment admitted no light, whether because it did not communicate with the outer world, or because night was fallen, he was unable to tell.

There were two doors in the room, one of very massive construction, and the other a smaller one. The place was dimly lighted by a brass lantern which hung from the ceiling. Harley stood up, staggered slightly, and then sat down again.

"My God," he groaned and raised his hand to his head.

For a few moments he remained seated, victim of a deadly nausea. Then, clenching his jaws grimly, again he stood up, and this time succeeded in reaching the heavy door.

As he had supposed, it was firmly locked, and a glance was sufficient to show him that his unaided effort could never force it. He turned his attention to the smaller door, which opened at his touch, revealing a sleeping apartment not unlike a monk's cell, adjoining which was a tiny bathroom. Neither rooms boasted windows, both being lighted by brass lanterns.

Harley examined them and their appointments with the utmost care, and then returned again to the outer room, one feature of which, and quite the most remarkable, he had reserved for special investigation.

This was a massive screen of gilded iron scroll work, which occupied nearly the whole of one end of the room. Beyond the screen hung a violet-coloured curtain of Oriental fabric; but so closely woven was the metal design that although he could touch this curtain with his finger at certain points, it proved impossible for him to move it aside in any way.

He noted that its lower fringe did not quite touch the door. By stooping down, he could see a few feet into some room beyond. It was in darkness, however, and beyond the fact that it was carpeted with a rich Persian rug, he learned but little from his scrutiny. The gilded screen was solid and immovable.

Nodding his head grimly, Harley felt in his pockets for pipe and pouch, wondering if these, too, had been taken from him. They had not, however, and the first nausea of his awakening having passed, he filled and lighted his briar and dropped down upon the divan to consider his position.

That it was fairly desperate was a fact he was unable to hide from himself, but at least he was still alive, which was a matter at once for congratulation and surprise.

He had noticed before, in raising his hand to his head, that his forehead felt cold and wet, and now, considering the matter closely, he came to the conclusion that an attempt had been made to aid his recovery, by some person or persons who must have retired at the moment that he had shown signs of returning consciousness.

His salvation, then, was not accidental but deliberate. He wondered what awaited him and why his life had been spared. That he had walked blindly into a trap prepared for him by that mysterious personality known as Fire-Tongue, he no longer could doubt. Intense anxiety and an egotistical faith in his own acumen had led him to underestimate the cleverness of his enemies, a vice from which ordinarily he was free.

From what hour they had taken a leading interest in his movements, he would probably never know, but that they had detected Paul Harley beneath the vendor of "Old Moore's Almanac" was certain enough. What a fool he had been!

He reproached himself bitterly. Ordinary common sense should have told him that the Hindu secretary had given those instructions to the chauffeur in the courtyard of the Savoy Hotel for his, Paul Harley's, special benefit. It was palpable enough now. He wondered how he had ever fallen into such a trap, and biting savagely upon his pipe, he strove to imagine what ordeal lay ahead of him.

So his thoughts ran, drifting from his personal danger, which he knew to be great, to other matters, which he dreaded to consider, because they meant far more to him than his own life. Upon these bitter reflections a slight sound intruded, the first which had disturbed the stillness about him since the moment of his awakening.

Someone had entered the room beyond the gilded screen, and now a faint light showed beneath the fringe of the curtain. Paul Harley sat quite still, smoking and watching.

He had learned to face the inevitable with composure, and now, apprehending the worst, he waited, puffing at his pipe. Presently he detected the sound of someone crossing the room toward him, or rather toward the screen. He lay back against the mattress which formed the back of the divan, and watched the gap below the curtain.

Suddenly he perceived a pair of glossy black boots. Their wearer was evidently standing quite near the screen, possibly listening. Harley had an idea that some second person stood immediately behind the first. Of this idea he presently had confirmation. He was gripping the stem of his pipe very tightly and any one who could have seen him sitting there must have perceived that although his face wore an unusual pallor, he was composed and entirely master of himself.

A voice uttered his name:

"Mr. Paul Harley."

He could not be sure, but he thought it was the voice of Ormuz Khan's secretary. He drew his pipe from between his teeth, and:

"Yes, what do you want with me?" he asked.

"Your attention, Mr. Harley, for a few moments, if you feel sufficiently recovered."

"Pray proceed," said Harley.

Of the presence of a second person beyond the screen he was now assured, for he had detected the sound of whispered instructions; and sinking lower and lower upon the divan, he peered surreptitiously under the border of the curtain, believing it to be more than probable that his movements were watched.

This led to a notable discovery. A pair of gray suede shoes became visible a few inches behind the glossy black boots—curiously small shoes with unusually high heels. The identity of their wearer was beyond dispute to the man who had measured that delicate foot.

Ormuz Khan stood behind the screen!

XXV

AN ENGLISHMAN'S HONOUR

"YOU HAVE BEEN guilty of a series of unfortunate mistakes, Mr. Harley," continued the speaker. "Notably, you have relied upon the clumsy device of disguise. To the organization in which you have chosen to interest yourself, this has provided some mild amusement. Your pedlar of almanacs was a clever impersonation, but fortunately your appearance at the Savoy had been anticipated, and no one was deceived."

Paul Harley did not reply. He concluded, quite correctly, that the organization had failed to detect himself in the person of the nervous cobbler. He drew courage from this deduction. Fire-Tongue was not omniscient.

"It is possible," continued the unseen speaker, in whom Harley had now definitely recognized Ormuz Khan's secretary, "that you recently overheard a resolution respecting yourself. Your death, in fact, had been determined upon. Life and death being synonymous, the philosopher contemplates either with equanimity."

"I am contemplating the latter with equanimity at the moment," said Harley, dryly.

"The brave man does so," the Hindu continued, smoothly. "The world only seems to grow older; its youth is really eternal, but as age succeeds age, new creeds must take the place of the old ones which are burned out. Fire, Mr. Harley, sweeps everything from its path irresistibly. You have dared to stand in the path of a fiery dawn; therefore, like all specks of dust which clog the wheels of progress, you must be brushed aside."

Harley nodded grimly, watching a ring of smoke floating slowly upward.

"It is a little thing to those who know the truth," the speaker resumed. "To the purblind laws of the West it may seem a great thing. We seek in Rome to do as Rome does. We judge every man as we find him. Therefore, recognizing that your total disappearance might compromise our movements in the near future, we have decided to offer you an alternative. This offer is based upon the British character. Where the oath of some men is a thing of smoke, the word of honour of an Englishman we are prepared to accept."

"Many thanks," murmured Harley. "On behalf of Great Britain I accept the compliment."

"We have such faith in the completeness of our plans, and in the nearness of the hour of triumph, that if you will pledge yourself to silence, in writing, you will not be molested in any way. You occupy at the moment the apartment reserved for neophytes of a certain order. But we do not ask you to become a neophyte. Disciples must seek us, we do not seek disciples. We only ask for your word that you will be silent."

"It is impossible," said Harley, tersely.

"Think well of the matter. It may not seem so impossible tomorrow."

"I decline definitely."

"You are sustaining yourself with false hopes, Mr. Harley. You think you have clues which will enable you to destroy a system rooted in the remote past. Also you forget that you have lost your freedom."

Paul Harley offered no further answer to the speaker concealed behind the violet curtain.

"Do not misunderstand us," the voice continued. "We bind you to nothing but silence."

"I refuse," said Harley, sharply. "Dismiss the matter."

"In spite of your refusal, time for consideration will be given to you."

Faintly Paul Harley detected the sounds made by Ormuz Khan and his secretary in withdrawing. The light beneath the curtain disappeared.

For perhaps a space of two hours, Paul Harley sat smoking and contemplating the situation from every conceivable angle. It was certainly desperate enough, and after a time he rose with a weary sigh, and made a second and more detailed examination of the several apartments.

It availed him nothing, but one point he definitely established. Escape was impossible, failing outside assistance. A certain coldness in the atmosphere, which was perceptible immediately beneath the barred window, led him to believe that this communicated with the outer air.

He was disposed to think that his unconsciousness had lasted less than an hour, and that it was still dark without. He was full of distrust. He no longer believed his immediate death to have been decided upon. For some reason it would seem that the group wished him to live, at any rate, temporarily. But now a complete theory touching the death of Sir Charles Abingdon had presented itself to his mind. Knowing little, but suspecting much of the resources of Fire-Tongue, he endeavoured to avoid contact with anything in the place.

Night attire was provided in the sleeping chamber, but he did not avail himself of this hospitality. Absolute silence reigned about him. Yet so immutable are Nature's laws, that presently Paul Harley sank back upon the mattresses, and fell asleep.

He awoke, acutely uncomfortable and ill-rested. He found a shaft of light streaming into the room, and casting shadows of the iron bars upon the opposite wall. The brass lantern still burned above him, and the silence remained complete as when he had fallen asleep. He stood up yawning and stretching himself.

At least, it was good to be still alive. He was vaguely conscious of the fact that he had been dreaming of Phil Abingdon, and suppressing a sigh, he clenched his teeth grimly and entered the little bathroom. There proved to be a plentiful supply of hot and cold water. At this he sniffed suspiciously, but at last:

"I'll risk it," he muttered.

He undressed and revelled in the joy of a hot bath, concluding with a cold plunge. A razor and excellent toilet requisites were set upon the dressing table, and whilst his imagination whispered that the soap might be poisoned and the razor possess a septic blade, he shaved, and having shaved, lighted his pipe and redressed himself at leisure.

He had nearly completed his toilet when a slight sound in the outer room arrested his attention. He turned sharply, stepping through the doorway.

A low carved table, the only one which the apartment boasted, displayed an excellent English breakfast laid upon a spotless cover.

"Ah," he murmured, and by the sight was mentally translated to that celebrated apartment of the palace at Versailles, where Louis XIV and his notorious favourite once were accustomed to dine, alone, and unsuitably dressed, the courses being served in just this fashion.

Harley held his pipe in his hand, and contemplated the repast. It was only logical to suppose it to be innocuous, and a keen appetite hastened the issue. He sidetracked his suspicion, and made an excellent breakfast. So the first day of his captivity began.

Growing used to the stillness about him, he presently began to detect, as the hours wore on, distant familiar sounds. Automobiles on the highroad, trains leaving and entering a tunnel which he judged to be from two to three miles distant; even human voices at long intervals.

The noises of an English countryside crept through the barred windows. Beyond a doubt he was in the house known as Hillside. Probably at night the lights of London could be seen from the garden. He was within ordinary telephone call of Chancery Lane. Yet he resumed his pipe and smiled philosophically. He had hoped to see the table disappear beneath the floor. As evidence that he was constantly watched, this had occurred during a brief visit which he had made to the bedroom in quest of matches.

When he returned the table was in its former place, but the cover had been removed. He carefully examined the floor beneath it, and realized that there was no hope of depressing the trap from above. Then, at an hour which he judged to be that of noon, the same voice addressed him from beyond the gilded screen.

"Mr. Paul Harley?"

"Yes, what have you to say?"

"By this time, Mr. Harley, you must have recognized that opposition is futile. At any moment we could visit death upon you. Escape, on the other hand, is out of the question. We desire you no harm. For diplomatic reasons, we should prefer you to live. Our cause is a sacred one. Do not misjudge it by minor incidents. A short statement and a copy of your English testament shall be placed upon the table, if you wish."

"I do not wish," Paul Harley returned.

"Is that your last word, Mr. Harley? We warn you that the third time of asking will be the last time."

"This is my last word."

"Your own life is not the only stake at issue."

"What do you mean?"

"You will learn what we mean, if you insist upon withholding your consent until we next invite it."

"Nevertheless, you may regard it as withheld, definitely and finally."

Silence fell, and Paul Harley knew himself to be once more alone. Luncheon appeared upon the table whilst he was washing in the bathroom. Remembering the change in the tone of the unseen speaker's voice, he avoided touching anything.

From the divan, through half-closed eyes, he examined every inch of the walls, seeking for the spy-hole through which he knew himself to be watched. He detected it at last: a little grating, like a ventilator, immediately above him where he sat. This communicated with some room where a silent watcher was constantly on duty!

Paul Harley gave no sign that he had made this discovery. But already his keen wits were at work upon a plan. He watched the bar of light fading, fading, until, judging it to be dinner time, he retired discreetly.

When he returned, he found dinner spread upon the table.

He wondered for what ordeal the neophyte was prepared in this singular apartment. He wondered how such neophytes were chosen, and to what tests they were submitted before being accepted as members of the bloodthirsty order. He could not even surmise.

Evidently no neophyte had been accepted on the previous night, unless there were other like chambers in the house. The occupants of the shuttered cars must therefore have been more advanced members. He spent the night in the little cell-like bedchamber, and his second day of captivity began as the first had begun.

For his dinner he had eaten nothing but bread and fruit. For his breakfast he ate an egg and drank water from the tap in the bathroom. His plan was now nearing completion. Only one point remained doubtful.

At noon the voice again addressed him from behind the gilded screen:

"Mr. Paul Harley?"

"Yes?"

"Your last opportunity has come. For your own future or for that of the world you seem to care little or nothing. Are you still determined to oppose our wishes?

"I am."

"You have yet an hour. Your final decision will be demanded of you at the end of that time."

Faint sounds of withdrawal followed these words and Harley suddenly discovered himself to be very cold. The note of danger had touched him. For long it had been silent. Now it clamoured insistently. He knew beyond all doubt that he was approaching a crisis in his life. At its nature he could not even guess.

He began to pace the room nervously, listening for he knew not what. His mind was filled with vague imaginings; when at last came an overture to the grim test to be imposed upon him.

A slight metallic sound drew his glance in the direction of the gilded screen. A sliding door of thick plate glass had been closed behind it, filling the space between the metal work and the curtain. Then—the light in the brass lantern became extinguished.

Standing rigidly, fists clenched, Paul Harley watched the curtain. And as he watched, slowly it was drawn aside. He found himself looking into a long room which appeared to be practically unfurnished.

The floor was spread with rugs and at the farther end folding doors had been opened, so that he could see into a second room, most elegantly appointed in Persian fashion. Here were silver lanterns, and many silken cushions, out of which, as from a sea of colour, arose slender pillars, the scheme possessing an air of exotic luxury peculiarly Oriental.

Seated in a carved chair over which a leopard skin had been thrown, and talking earnestly to some invisible companion, whose conversation seemed wholly to enthrall her, was Phil Abingdon!

XXVI

THE ORCHID OF SLEEP

"MY GOD!" cried Innes, "here is proof that the chief was right!"

Wessex nodded in silent agreement. On the table lay the report of Merton, the analyst, concerning the stains upon the serviette which Harley had sent from the house of the late Sir Charles Abingdon. Briefly, it stated that the serviette had been sprinkled with some essential oil, the exact character of which Merton had found himself unable to determine, its perfume, if it ever possessed any, having disappeared. And the minute quantity obtainable from the linen rendered ordinary tests difficult to apply. The analyst's report, however, concluded as follows:

> Mr. Harley, having foreseen these difficulties, and having apparently suspected that the oil was of Oriental origin, recommended me, in the note which he enclosed with the serviette, to confer with Dr. Warwick Grey. I send a copy of a highly interesting letter which I have received from Doctor Grey, whose knowledge of Eastern poison is unparalleled, and to whose opinion I attach immense importance.

It was the contents of this appended letter which had inspired Innes's remarks. Indeed, it contained matter which triumphantly established Paul Harley's theory that Sir Charles Abingdon had not died from natural causes. The letter was as follows:

> Number 435, Harley Street London, W. I.
>
> My Dear Merton:
>
> I am indebted to you and to Mr. Harley for an opportunity of examining the serviette, which I return herewith. I agree that the oil does not respond to ordinary tests, nor is any smell perceptible. But you have noticed in your microscopic examination of the stains that there is a peculiar crystalline formation upon the surface. You state that this is quite unfamiliar to you, which is not at all strange, since outside of the Himalayan districts of Northwest India I have never met with it myself.
>
> Respecting the character of the oil employed, however, I am in no doubt, and I actually possess a dried specimen of the flower from which it is expressed. This is poetically known among the Mangars, one of the fighting tribes or Nepal, as the Bloom or Orchid of Sleep.
>
> It is found upon the lower Himalayan slopes, and bears a close resemblance to the white odontoglossum of commerce, except that the flower is much smaller. Its perfume attracts insects

and sometimes small animals and reptiles, although inhalation seems to induce instant death. It may be detected in its natural state by the presence of hundreds of dead flies and insects upon the ground surrounding the plant. It is especially fatal to nocturnal insects, its perfume being stronger at night.

Preparation of the oil is an art peculiar to members of an obscure sect established in that district, by whom it is said to be employed for the removal of enemies.

An article is sprinkled with it, and whilst the perfume, which is reported to resemble that of cloves, remains perceptible, to inhale it results in immediate syncope, although by what physiological process I have never been enabled to determine.

With the one exception which I have mentioned, during my stay in Nepal and the surrounding districts I failed to obtain a specimen of this orchid. I have twice seen the curious purple stain upon articles of clothing worn by natives who had died suddenly and mysteriously. The Mangars simply say, "He has offended someone. It is the flower of sleep."

I immediately recognized the colour of the stains upon the enclosed serviette, and also the curious crystalline formation on their surface. The identity of the "someone" to whom the Mangars refer, I never established. I shall welcome any particulars respecting the history of the serviette.

Very truly yours,
Warwick Grey.

"Sir Charles Abingdon was poisoned," said Wessex in a hushed voice. "For the girl's sake I hate the idea, but we shall have to get an exhumation order."

"It is impossible," returned Innes, shortly. "He was cremated."

"Good heavens," murmured Wessex, "I never knew."

"But after all," continued Inures, "it is just as well for everyone concerned. The known facts are sufficient to establish the murder, together with the report of Dr. Warwick Grey. But, meanwhile, are we any nearer to learning the identity of the murderer?"

"We are not!" said Wessex, grimly. "And what's more, when I get to Scotland Yard, I have got to face the music. First Mr. Harley goes, and now Nicol Brinn has disappeared!"

"It's almost unbelievable!"

"I took him for a white man," said the detective, earnestly. "I accepted his parole for twenty-four hours. The twenty-four hours expired about noon today, but since he played that trick on Stokes last night and went out of his chambers, he has vanished utterly."

Innes stood up excitedly.

"Your ideas may be all wrong, Wessex!" he cried. "Don't you see that he may have gone the same way as the chief?"

"He was mightily anxious to get out, at any rate."

"And you have no idea where he went?"

"Not the slightest. Following his performance of last night, of course I was compelled to instal a man in the chambers, and this morning someone rang up from the house of Lord Wolverham; he is commanding officer of one of the Guards battalions, I believe. It appears that Mr. Nicol Brinn not only locked up a representative of the Criminal Investigation Department, but also stole a Rolls Royce car from outside the Cavalry Club!"

"What!" cried Innes. "Stole a car?"

"Stole Lord Wolverham's car and calmly drove away in it. We have failed to trace both car and man!" The detective inspector sighed wearily. "Well, I suppose I must get along to the Yard. Stokes has got the laugh on me this time."

Wearing a very gloomy expression, the detective inspector proceeded on foot to New Scotland Yard, and being informed on his arrival upstairs that the Assistant Commissioner was expecting him, he entered the office of that great man.

The Assistant Commissioner, who had palpably seen military service, was a big man with very tired eyes, and a quiet, almost apologetic manner.

"Ah, Detective Inspector," he said, as Wessex entered. "I wanted to see you about this business of Mr. Nicol Brinn."

"Yes, sir," replied Wessex, "naturally."

"Now," the Assistant Commissioner turned wearily in his chair, and glanced up at his subordinate—"your accepting the parole of a suspect, under the circumstances, was officially improper, but I am not blaming you—I am not blaming you for a moment. Mr. Nicol Brinn's well-known reputation justified your behaviour." He laid one large hand firmly upon the table. "Mr. Nicol Brinn's absence alters the matter entirely."

"I am well aware of it," murmured the inspector. "Although," continued the Assistant Commissioner, "Mr. Brinn's record leads me to believe that he will have some suitable explanation to offer, his behaviour, you will admit, is that of a guilty man?"

"It is, sir; it certainly is."

"The Press, fortunately, has learned nothing of this unpleasant business, particularly unpleasant because it involves such well-known people. You will see to it, Detective Inspector, that all publicity is avoided if possible. Meanwhile, as a matter of ordinary departmental routine, you will circulate Mr. Brinn's description through the usual channels, and—" the Assistant Commissioner raised his eyebrows slightly.

"You mean that?" asked Wessex.

"Certainly. He must be arrested by the first officer who recognizes him."

"Very good, sir. I will move in the matter at once."

"Do so, please." The Assistant Commissioner sighed wearily, as one of his telephones set up a muted buzzing. "That is all for the moment, I think. Good morning."

Detective Inspector Wessex came out, quietly closing the door behind him. He felt that he had been let down very lightly. But nevertheless he was unpleasantly warm, and as he walked slowly along the corridor he whistled softly, and:

"Arrest of Mr. Nicol Brinn," he muttered. "What a headline, if they ever get it!"

XXVII

AT HILLSIDE

PHIL ABINGDON ARRIVED at Hillside in a state of mind which she found herself unable to understand. Mrs. McMurdoch, who had accepted the invitation under protest, saying that if Doctor McMurdoch had been at home he would certainly have disapproved, had so utterly fallen under the strange spell of Ormuz Khan, that long before they had come to Hillside she was hanging upon his every word in a way which was almost pathetic to watch.

On the other hand, Phil Abingdon had taken up a definite attitude of defense; and perceiving this, because of his uncanny intuitiveness, the Persian had exerted himself to the utmost, more often addressing Phil than her companion, and striving to regain that mastery of her emotions which he had formerly achieved, at least in part.

Her feelings, however, were largely compounded of fear, and fear strengthened her defense. The repulsive part of Ormuz Khan's character became more apparent to her than did the fascination which she had once experienced. She distrusted him, distrusted him keenly. She knew at the bottom of her heart that this had always been so, but she had suffered his attentions in much the same spirit as that which imbues the naturalist who studies the habits of a poisonous reptile.

She knew that she was playing with fire, and in this knowledge lay a dangerous pleasure. She had the utmost faith in her own common sense, and was ambitious to fence with edged tools.

When at last the car was drawn up before the porch of Hillside, and Ormuz Khan, stepping out, assisted the ladies to alight, for one moment Phil Abingdon hesitated, although she knew that it was already too late to do so. They were received by Mr. Rama Dass, his excellency's courteous secretary, whom she had already met, and whom Ormuz Khan presented to Mrs. McMurdoch. Almost immediately:

"You have missed Mr. Harley by only a few minutes," said Rama Dass.

"What!" exclaimed Phil, her eyes opening very widely.

"Oh, there is no occasion for alarm," explained the secretary in his urbane manner. "He has ventured as far as Lower Claybury station. The visit was unavoidable. He particularly requested that we should commence luncheon, but hoped to be back before we should have finished."

Phil Abingdon glanced rapidly from the face of the speaker to that of Ormuz Khan. But her scrutiny of those unreadable countenances availed her nothing. She was conscious of a great and growing uneasiness; and Mrs. McMurdoch, misunderstanding the expression upon her face, squeezed her arm playfully.

"Cheer up, dear," she whispered. "He will be here soon!"

Phil knew that her face had flushed deeply. Partly she was glad of her emotions, and partly ashamed. This sweet embarrassment in which there was a sort of pain was a new experience, but one wholly delightful. She laughed, and accepting the arm of Ormuz Khan, walked into a very English-looking library, followed by Rama Dass and Mrs. McMurdoch. The house, she thought, was very silent, and she found herself wondering why no servants had appeared.

Rama Dass had taken charge of the ladies' cloaks in the hall, and in spite of the typical English environment in which she found herself, Phil sat very near to Mrs. McMurdoch on a settee, scarcely listening to the conversation, and taking no part in it.

For there was a strange and disturbing air of loneliness about Hillside. She would have welcomed the appearance of a butler or a parlourmaid, or any representative of the white race. Yes: there lay the root of the matter—this feeling of aloofness from all that was occidental, a feeling which the English appointments of the room did nothing to dispel. Then a gong sounded and the party went in to lunch.

A white-robed Hindu waited at table, and Phil discovered his movements to be unpleasantly silent. There was something very unreal about it all. She found herself constantly listening for the sound of an approaching car, of a footstep, of a voice, the voice of Paul Harley. This waiting presently grew unendurable, and:

"I hope Mr. Harley is safe," she said, in a rather unnatural tone. "Surely he should have returned by now?"

Ormuz Khan shrugged his slight shoulders and glanced at a diamond-studded wrist watch which he wore.

"There is nothing to fear," he declared, in his soft, musical voice. "He knows how to take care of himself. And"—with a significant glance of his long, magnetic eyes—"I am certain he will return as speedily as possible."

Nevertheless, luncheon terminated, and Harley had not appeared.

"You have sometimes expressed a desire," said Ormuz Khan, "to see the interior of a Persian house. Permit me to show you the only really characteristic room which I allow myself in my English home."

Endeavouring to conceal her great anxiety, Phil allowed herself to be conducted by the Persian to an apartment which realized her dreams of that Orient which she had never visited.

Three beautiful silver lanterns depended from a domed ceiling in which wonderfully woven tapestry was draped. The windows were partly obscured by carved wooden screens, and the light entered through little panels of coloured glass. There were cushioned divans, exquisite pottery, and a playful fountain plashing in a marble pool.

Ormuz Khan conducted her to a wonderfully carven chair over which a leopard's skin was draped and there she seated herself. She saw through a wide doorway before her a long and apparently unfurnished room dimly lighted. At the farther end she could vaguely discern violet-coloured draperies. Ormuz Khan gracefully threw himself upon a divan to the right of this open door.

"This, Miss Abingdon," he said, "is a nearly exact reproduction of a room of a house which I have in Ispahan. I do not claim that it is typical, but does its manner appeal to you?"

"Immensely," she replied, looking around her.

She became aware of a heavy perfume of hyacinths, and presently observed that there were many bowls of those flowers set upon little tables, and in niches in the wall.

"Yet its atmosphere is not truly of the Orient."

"Are such apartments uncommon, then, in Persia?" asked Phil, striving valiantly to interest herself in the conversation.

"I do not say so," he returned, crossing one delicate foot over the other, in languorous fashion. "But many things which are typically of the Orient would probably disillusion you, Miss Abingdon."

"In what way?" she asked, wondering why Mrs. McMurdoch had not joined them.

"In many subtle ways. The real wonder and the mystery of the East lie not upon the surface, but beneath it. And beneath the East of today lies the East of yesterday."

The speaker's expression grew rapt, and he spoke in the mystic manner which she knew and now dreaded. Her anxiety for the return of Paul Harley grew urgent—a positive need, as, meeting the gaze of the long, magnetic eyes, she felt again, like the touch of cold steel, all the penetrating force of this man's will. She was angrily aware of the fact that his gaze was holding hers hypnotically, that she was meeting it contrary to her wish and inclination. She wanted to look away but found herself looking steadily into the coal-black eyes of Ormuz Khan.

"The East of yesterday"—his haunting voice seemed to reach her from a great distance—"saw the birth of all human knowledge and human power; and to us the East of yesterday is the East of today."

Phil became aware that a sort of dreamy abstraction was creeping over her, when in upon this mood came a sound which stimulated her weakening powers of resistance.

Dimly, for all the windows of the room were closed, she heard a car come up and stop before the house. It aroused her from the curious condition of lethargy into which she was falling. She turned her head sharply aside, the physical reflection of a mental effort to remove her gaze from the long, magnetic eyes of Ormuz Khan. And:

"Do you think that is Mr. Harley?" she asked, and failed to recognize her own voice.

"Possibly," returned the Persian, speaking very gently.

With one ivory hand he touched his knee for a moment, the only expression of disappointment which he allowed himself.

"May I ask you to go and enquire?" continued Phil, now wholly mistress of herself again. "I am wondering, too, what can have become of Mrs. McMurdoch."

"I will find out," said Ormuz Khan.

He rose, his every movement possessing a sort of feline grace. He bowed and walked out of the room. Phil Abingdon heard in the distance the motor restarted and the car being driven away from Hillside. She stood up restlessly.

Beneath the calm of the Persian's manner she had detected the presence of dangerous fires. The silence of the house oppressed her. She was not actually frightened yet, but intuitively she knew that all was not well. Then came a new sound arousing active fear at last.

Someone was rapping upon one of the long, masked windows! Phil Abingdon started back with a smothered exclamation.

"Quick!" came a high, cool voice, "open this window. You are in danger."

The voice was odd, peculiar, but of one thing she was certain. It was not the voice of an Oriental; Furthermore, it held a note of command, and something, too, which inspired trust.

She looked quickly about her to make sure that she was alone. And then, running swiftly to the window from which the sound had come, she moved a heavy gilded fastening which closed it, and drew open the heavy leaves.

A narrow terrace was revealed with a shrubbery beyond; and standing on the terrace was a tall, thin man wearing a light coat over evening dress. He looked pale, gaunt, and unshaven, and although the regard of his light eyes was almost dreamy, there was something very tense in his pose.

"I am Nicol Brinn," said the stranger. "I knew your father. You have walked into a trap. I am here to get you out of it. Can you drive?"

"Do you mean an automobile?" asked Phil, breathlessly.

"A Rolls Royce."

"Yes."

"Come right out."

"My furs! my hat!"

"Something bigger is at stake."

It was all wildly bizarre, almost unbelievable. Phil Abingdon had experienced in her own person the insidious power of Ormuz Khan. She now found herself under the spell of a personality at least as forceful, although in a totally different way. She found herself running through a winding path amid bushes, piloted by this strange, unshaven man, to whom on sight she had given her trust unquestioningly!

"When we reach the car," he said over his shoulder, "ask no questions—head for home, and don't stop for anything—on two legs or on four. That's the first thing—most important; then, when you know you're safe, telephone Scotland Yard to send a raid squad down by road, and do it quick."

XXVIII

THE CHASE

THE EVENTS WHICH led to the presence of Mr. Nicol Brinn at so opportune a moment were—consistent with the character of that remarkable man—of a sensational nature.

Having commandeered the Rolls Royce from the door of the Cavalry Club, he had immediately, by a mental process which many perils had perfected, dismissed the question of rightful ownership from his mind. The fact that he might be intercepted by police scouts he refused to entertain. The limousine driven by the Hindu chauffeur was still in sight, and until Mr. Nicol Brinn had seen it garaged, nothing else mattered, nothing else counted, and nothing else must be permitted to interfere.

Jamming his hat tightly upon his head, he settled down at the wheel, drawing up rather closer to the limousine as the chase lay through crowded thoroughfares and keeping his quarry comfortably in sight across Westminster Bridge and through the outskirts of London.

He had carefully timed the drive to the unknown abode of Fire-Tongue, and unless it had been prolonged, the more completely to deceive him, he had determined that the house lay not more than twenty miles from Piccadilly.

When Mitcham was passed, and the limousine headed straight on into Surrey, he decided that there had been no doubling, but that the house to which he had been taken lay in one of these unsuspected country backwaters, which, while they are literally within sight of the lights of London, have nevertheless a remoteness as complete as secrecy could desire.

It was the deserted country roads which he feared, for if the man ahead of him should suspect pursuit, a difficult problem might arise.

By happy chance Nicol Brinn, an enthusiastic motorist, knew the map of Surrey as few Englishmen knew it. Indeed, there was no beauty spot within a forty-mile radius of London to which he could not have driven by the best and shortest route, at a moment's notice. This knowledge aided him now.

For presently at a fork in the road he saw that the driver of the limousine had swung to the left, taking the low road, that to the right offering a steep gradient. The high road was the direct road to Lower Claybury, the low road a detour to the same.

Nicol Brinn mentally reviewed the intervening countryside, and taking a gambler's chance, took the Rolls Royce up the hill. He knew exactly what he was about, and he knew that the powerful engine would eat up the slope with ease.

Its behaviour exceeded his expectations, and he found himself mounting the acclivity at racing speed. At its highest point, the road, skirting a hilltop, offered an extensive view of the valley below. Here Nicol Brinn pulled up and, descending, watched and listened.

In the stillness he could plainly hear the other automobile humming steadily along the lowland road below. He concentrated his mind upon the latter part of that strange journey, striving to recall any details which had marked it immediately preceding the time when he had detected the rustling of leaves and knew that they had entered a carriage drive.

Yes, there had been a short but steep hill; and immediately before this the car had passed over a deeply rutted road, or—he had a sudden inspiration—over a level crossing.

He knew of just such a hilly road immediately behind Lower Claybury station. Indeed, it was that by which he should be compelled to descend if he continued to pursue his present route to the town. He could think of no large, detached house, the Manor Park excepted, which corresponded to the one which he sought. But that in taking the high road he had acted even more wisely than he knew, he was now firmly convinced.

He determined to proceed as far as the park gates as speedily as possible. Therefore, returning to the wheel, he sent the car along the now level road at top speed, so that the railings of the Manor Park, when presently he found himself skirting the grounds, had the semblance of a continuous iron fence wherever the moonlight touched them.

He passed the head of the road dipping down to Lower Claybury, but forty yards beyond pulled up and descended. Again he stood listening, and:

"Good!" he muttered.

He could hear the other car labouring up the slope. He ran along to the corner of the lane, and, crouching close under the bushes, waited for its appearance. As he had supposed, the chauffeur turned the car to the right.

"Good!" muttered Nicol Brinn again.

There was a baggage-rack immediately above the number plate. Upon this Nicol Brinn sprang with the agility of a wildcat, settling himself upon his perilous perch before the engine had had time to gather speed.

When presently the car turned into the drive of Hillside, Nicol Brinn dropped off and dived into the bushes on the right of the path. From this hiding place he saw the automobile driven around the front of the house to the garage, which was built out from the east wing. Not daring to pursue his investigations until the chauffeur had retired, he sought a more comfortable spot near a corner of the lawn and there, behind a bank of neglected flowers, lay down, watching the man's shadowy figure moving about in the garage.

Although he was some distance from the doors he could see that there was a second car in the place—a low, torpedo-bodied racer, painted battleship gray. This sight turned his thoughts in another direction.

Very cautiously he withdrew to the drive again, retracing his steps to the lane, and walking back to the spot where he had left the Rolls Royce, all the time peering about him to right and left. He was looking for a temporary garage for the car, but one from which, if necessary, he could depart in a hurry. The shell of an ancient barn, roofless and desolate, presently invited inspection and, as a result, a few minutes later Colonel Lord Wolverham's luxurious automobile was housed for the night in these strange quarters.

When Nicol Brinn returned to Hillside, he found the garage locked and the lights extinguished. Standing under a moss-grown wall which sheltered him from the house, from his case he selected a long black cigar, lighted it with care and, having his hands thrust in the pockets of his light overcoat and the cigar protruding aggressively from the left corner of his mouth, he moved along to an angle of the wall and stared reflectively at the silent house.

A mental picture arose of a secret temple in the shadow of the distant Himalayas. Was it credible that this quiet country house, so typical of rural England, harboured that same dread secret which he had believed to be locked away in those Indian hills? Could he believe that the dark and death-dealing power which he had seen at work in the East was now centred here, within telephone-call of London?

The fate of Sir Charles Abingdon and of Paul Harley would seem to indicate that such was the case. Beyond doubt, the document of which Rama Dass had spoken was some paper in the possession of the late Sir Charles. Much that had been mysterious was cleared up. He wondered why it had not occurred to him from the first that Sir Charles's inquiry, which he had mentioned to Paul Harley, respecting Fire-Tongue, had been due to the fact that the surgeon had seen the secret mark upon his arm after the accident in the Haymarket. He remembered distinctly that his sleeve had been torn upon that occasion. He could not imagine, however, what had directed the attention of the organization to Sir Charles, and for what reason his death had been decided upon.

He rolled his cigar from corner to corner of his mouth, staring reflectively with lack-lustre eyes at the silent house before him. In the moonlight it made a peaceful picture enough. A cautious tour of the place revealed a lighted window upon the first floor. Standing in the shadow of an old apple tree, Nicol Brinn watched the blind of this window minute after minute, patiently waiting for a shadow to appear upon it; and at last his patience was rewarded.

A shadow appeared—the shadow of a woman!

Nicol Brinn dropped his cigar at his feet and set his heel upon it. A bitter-sweet memory which had been with him for seven years arose again in his mind. There is a kind of mountain owl in certain parts of northern India which possesses a curiously high, plaintive note. He wondered if he could remember and reproduce that note.

He made the attempt, repeating the cry three times. At the third repetition the light in the first floor window went out. He heard the sound of the window being gently opened. Then a voice—a voice which held the sweetest music in the world for the man who listened below—spoke softly:

"Nicol!"

"Naida!" he called. "Come down to me. You must. Don't answer. I will wait here."

"Promise you will let me return!"

He hesitated.

"Promise!"

"I promise."

XXIX

THE CATASTROPHE

THE FIRST FAINT spears of morning creeping through the trees which surrounded Hillside revealed two figures upon a rustic bench in the little orchard adjoining the house. A pair incongruous enough—this dark-eyed Eastern woman, wrapped in a long fur cloak, and Nicol Brinn, gaunt, unshaven, fantastic in his evening dress, revealed now in the gray morning light.

"Look!" whispered Naida. "It is the dawn. I must go!"

Nicol Brinn clenched his teeth tightly but made no reply.

"You promised," she said, and although her voice was very tender she strove to detach his arm, which was locked about her shoulders.

He nodded grimly.

"I'll keep my word. I made a contract with hell with my eyes open, and I'll stick to it." He stood up suddenly. "Go back, Naida!" he said. "Go back! You have my promise, now, and I'm helpless. But at last I see a way, and I'm going to take it."

"What do you mean?" she cried, standing up and clutching his arm.

"Never mind." His tone was cool again. "Just go back."

"You would not—" she began.

"I never broke my word in my life, and even now I'm not going to begin. While you live I stay silent."

In the growing light Naida looked about her affrightedly. Then, throwing her arms impulsively around Brinn, she kissed him—a caress that was passionate but sexless; rather the kiss of a mother who parts with a beloved son than that which a woman bestows upon the man she loves; an act of renunciation.

He uttered a low cry and would have seized her in his arms but, lithely evading him, she turned, stifling a sob, and darted away through the trees toward the house.

For long he stood looking after her, fists clenched and his face very gray in the morning light. Some small inner voice told him that his new plan, and the others which he had built upon it, must crumble and fall as a castle of sand. He groaned and, turning aside, made his way through the shrubbery to the highroad.

He was become accessory to a murder; for he had learned for what reason and by what means Sir Charles Abingdon had been assassinated. He had even learned the identity of his assassin; had learned that the dreaded being called Fire-Tongue in India was known and respected throughout the civilized world as His Excellency Ormuz Khan!

Paul Harley had learned these things also, and now at this very hour Paul Harley lay a captive in Hillside. Naida had assured him that Paul Harley was alive and safe. It had been decided that his death would lead to the destruction of the movement, but pressure was being brought upon him to ensure his silence.

Yes, he, Nicol Brinn, was bound and manacled to a gang of assassins; and because his tongue was tied, because the woman he loved better than anything in the world was actually a member of the murderous group, he must pace the deserted country lanes inactive; he must hold his hand, although he might summon the resources of New Scotland Yard by phoning from Lower Claybury station!

Through life his word had been his bond, and Nicol Brinn was incapable of compromising with his conscience. But the direct way was barred to him. Nevertheless, no task could appal the inflexible spirit of the man, and he had registered a silent vow that Ormuz Khan should never leave England alive.

Not a soul was astir yet upon the country roads, and sitting down upon a grassy bank, Nicol Brinn lighted one of his black cigars, which in times of stress were his food and drink, upon which if necessary he could carry-on for forty-eight hours upon end.

In connection with his plan for coercing Harley, Ormuz Khan had gone to London by rail on the previous night, departing from Lower Claybury station at about the time that Colonel Lord Wolverham came out of the Cavalry Club to discover his Rolls Royce to be missing. This same Rolls Royce was now a source of some anxiety to Nicol Brinn, for its discovery by a passing labourer in the deserted barn seemed highly probable.

However, he had matters of greater urgency to think about, not the least of these being the necessity of concealing his presence in the neighbourhood of Hillside. Perhaps his Sioux-like face reflected a spirit allied in some respects to that of the once great Indian tribe.

His genius for taking cover, perfected upon many a big-game expedition, enabled him successfully to accomplish the feat; so that, when the limousine, which he had watched go by during the morning, returned shortly after noon, the lack-lustre eyes were peering out through the bushes near the entrance to the drive.

Instinct told him that the pretty girl with whom Ormuz Khan was deep in conversation could be none other than Phil Abingdon, but the identity of her companion he could not even guess. On the other hand, that this poisonously handsome Hindu, who bent forward so solicitously toward his charming travelling companion, was none other than the dreaded Fire-Tongue, he did not doubt.

He returned to a strategic position which he had discovered during the night. In a measure he was nonplussed. That the presence of the girl was primarily associated with the coercion of Paul Harley, he understood; but might it not portend something even more sinister?

When, later, the limousine departed again, at great risk of detection he ran across a corner of the lawn to peer out into the lane, in order that he might obtain a glimpse of its occupant. This proved to be none other than Phil Abingdon's elderly companion. She had apparently been taken ill, and a dignified Hindu gentleman, wearing gold-rimmed pince-nez, was in attendance.

Nicol Brinn clenched his jaws hard. The girl had fallen into a trap. He turned rapidly, facing the house. Only at one point did the shrubbery approach the wall, but for that point he set out hot foot, passing from bush to bush with Indian cleverness, tense, alert, and cool in despite of his long vigil.

At last he came to the shallow veranda with its four sightless windows backed by fancifully carven screens. He stepped up to the first of these and pressed his ear against the glass.

Fate was with him, for almost immediately he detected a smooth, musical voice speaking in the room beyond. A woman's voice answered and, listening intently, he detected the sound of a closing door.

Thereupon he acted: with the result, as has appeared, that Phil Abingdon, hatless, without her furs, breathless and more frightened than she had ever been in her life, presently found herself driving a luxurious Rolls Royce out of a roofless barn on to the highroad, and down the slope to Claybury station.

It was at about this time, or a little later, that Paul Harley put into execution a project which he had formed. The ventilator above the divan, which he had determined to be the spy-hole through which his every movement was watched, had an ornamental framework studded with metal knobs. He had recently discovered an electric bell-push in the centre panel of the massive door of his prison.

Inwardly on fire, imagining a thousand and one horrors centring about the figure of Phil Abingdon, but retaining his outward calm by dint of a giant effort, he pressed this bell and waited.

Perhaps two minutes elapsed. Then the glass doors beyond the gilded screen were drawn open, and the now-familiar voice spoke:

"Mr. Paul Harley?"

"Yes," he replied, "I have made my final decision."

"And that is?"

"I agree."

"You are wise," the voice replied. "A statement will be placed before you for signature. When you have signed it, ring the bell again, and in a few minutes you will be free."

Vaguely he detected the speaker withdrawing. Thereupon, heaving a loud sigh, he removed his coat, looked about him as if in quest of some place to hang it, and finally, fixing his gaze upon the studded grating, stood upon the divan and hung his coat over the spy-hole! This accomplished, he turned.

The table was slowly sinking through the gap in the floor beneath.

Treading softly, he moved forward and seated himself cross-legged upon it! It continued to descend, and he found himself in absolute darkness.

* * *

Nicol Brinn ran on to the veranda and paused for a moment to take breath. The window remained open, as Phil Abingdon had left it. He stepped into the room with its elegant Persian appointments. It was empty. But as he crossed the threshold, he paused, arrested by the sound of a voice.

"A statement will be placed before you," said the voice, "and when you have signed it, in a few minutes you will be free."

Nicol Brinn silently dropped flat at the back of a divan, as Rama Dass, coming out of the room which communicated with the golden screen, made his way toward the distant door. Having one eye raised above the top of the cushions, Nicol Brinn watched him, recognizing the man who had accompanied the swooning lady. She had been deposited, then, at no great distance from the house.

He was to learn later that poor Mrs. McMurdoch, in her artificially induced swoon, had been left in charge of a hospitable cottager, while her solicitous Oriental escort had sped away in quest of a physician. But at the moment matters of even greater urgency engaged his attention.

Creeping forward to the doorway by which Rama Dass had gone out, Nicol Brinn emerged upon a landing from which stairs both ascended and descended. Faint sounds of footsteps below guided him, and although from all outward seeming he appeared to saunter casually down, his left hand was clutching the butt of a Colt automatic.

He presently found himself in a maze of basements—kitchens of the establishment, no doubt. The sound of footsteps no longer guided him. He walked along, and in a smaller deserted pantry discovered the base of a lift shaft in which some sort of small elevator worked. He was staring at this reflectively, when, for the second time in his adventurous career, a silken cord was slipped tightly about his throat!

He was tripped and thrown. He fought furiously, but the fatal knee pressure came upon his spine so shrewdly as to deprive him of the strength to raise his hands.

"My finish!" were the words that flashed through his mind, as sounds like the waves of a great ocean beat upon his ears and darkness began to descend.

Then, miraculously, the pressure ceased; the sound of great waters subsided; and choking, coughing, he fought his way back to life, groping like a blind man and striving to regain his feet.

"Mr. Brinn!" said a vaguely familiar voice. "Mr. Brinn!"

The realities reasserted themselves. Before him, pale, wide-eyed, and breathing heavily, stood Paul Harley; and prone upon the floor of the pantry lay Rama Dass, still clutching one end of the silken rope in his hand!

"Mr. Harley!" gasped Brinn. "My God, sir!" He clutched at his bruised throat. "I have to thank you for my life."

He paused, looking down at the prone figure as Harley, dropping upon his knees, turned the man over.

"I struck him behind the ear," he muttered, "and gave him every ounce. Good heavens!"

He had slipped his hand inside Rama Dass's vest, and now he looked up, his face very grim.

"Good enough!" said Brinn, coolly. "He asked for it; he's got it. Take this." He thrust the Colt automatic into Harley's hand as the latter stood up again.

"What do we do now?" asked Harley.

"Search the house," was the reply. "Everything coloured you see, shoot, unless I say no."

"Miss Abingdon?"

"She's safe. Follow me."

Straight up two flights of stairs led Nicol Brinn, taking three steps at a stride. Palpably enough the place was deserted. Ormuz Khan's plans for departure were complete.

Into two rooms on the first floor they burst, to find them stripped and bare. On the threshold of the third Brinn stopped dead, and his gaunt face grew ashen. Then he tottered across the room, arms outstretched.

"Naida," he whispered. "My love, my love!"

Paul Harley withdrew quietly. He had begun to walk along the corridor when the sound of a motor brought him up sharply. A limousine was being driven away from the side entrance! Not alone had he heard that sound. His face deathly, and the lack-lustre eyes dully on fire, Nicol Brinn burst out of the room and, not heeding the presence of Harley, hurled himself down the stairs. He was as a man demented, an avenging angel.

"There he is!" cried Harley—"heading for the Dover Road!"

Nicol Brinn, at the wheel of the racer—the same in which Harley had made his fateful journey and which had afterward been concealed in the garage at Hillside—scarcely nodded.

Nearer they drew to the quarry, and nearer. Once—twice—and again, the face of Ormuz Khan peered out of the window at the rear of the limousine.

They drew abreast; the road was deserted. And they passed slightly ahead.

Paul Harley glanced at the granite face of his companion with an apprehension he was unable to conceal. This was a cool madman who drove. What did he intend to do?

Inch by inch, Nicol Brinn edged the torpedo body nearer to the wheels of the racing limousine. The Oriental chauffeur drew in ever closer to the ditch bordering the roadside. He shouted hoarsely and was about to apply the brakes when the two cars touched!

A rending crash came—a hoarse scream—and the big limousine toppled over into the ditch.

Harley felt himself hurled through space.

"Shall I follow on to Lower Claybury, sir?" asked Inspector Wessex, excitedly.

Phil Abingdon's message had come through nearly an hour before, and a party had been despatched in accordance with Brinn's instructions. Wessex had returned to New Scotland Yard too late to take charge, and now, before the Assistant Commissioner had time to reply, a 'phone buzzed.

"Yes?" said the Assistant Commissioner, taking up one of the several instruments: "What!"

Even this great man, so justly celebrated for his placid demeanour, was unable to conceal his amazement.

"Yes," he added. "Let him come up!" He replaced the receiver and turning to Wessex: "Mr. Nicol Brinn is here!" he informed him.

"What's that!" cried the inspector, quite startled out of his usual deferential manner.

Footsteps sounded in the corridor. Came a rap at the door.

"Come in," said the Assistant Commissioner.

The door was thrown open and Nicol Brinn entered. One who knew him well would have said that he had aged ten years. Even to the eye of Wessex he looked an older man. He wore a shoddy suit and a rough tweed cap and his left arm was bandaged.

"Gentlemen," he said, without other greeting, "I'm here to make a statement. I desire that a shorthand-writer attend to take it down."

He dropped weakly into a chair which Wessex placed for him. The Assistant Commissioner, doubtless stimulated by the manner of his extraordinary visitor, who now extracted a cigar from the breast pocket of his ill-fitting jacket and nonchalantly lighted it, successfully resumed his well-known tired manner, and, pressing a bell:

"One shall attend, Mr. Brinn," he said.

A knock came at the door and a sergeant entered.

"Send Ferris," directed the Assistant Commissioner. "Quickly."

Two minutes later a man came in carrying a note book and fountain pen. The Assistant Commissioner motioned him to a chair, and:

"Pray proceed, Mr. Brinn," he said.

XXX

NICOL BRINN'S STORY OF THE CITY OF FIRE

"THE STATEMENT WHICH I have to make, gentlemen, will almost certainly appear incredible to you. However, when it has been transcribed I will sign it. And I am going to say here and now that there are points in the narrative which I am in a position to substantiate. What I can't prove you must take my word for. But I warn you that the story is tough.

"I have a certain reputation for recklessness. I don't say it may not be inherent; but if you care to look the matter up, you will find that the craziest phase of my life is that covering the last seven years. The reason why I have courted death during that period I am now about to explain.

"Although my father was no traveller, I think I was born with the wanderlust. I started to explore the world in my Harvard vacations, and when college days were over I set about the business wholeheartedly. Where I went and what I did, up to the time that my travels led me to India, is of no interest to you or to anybody else, be- cause in India I found heaven and hell—a discovery enough to satisfy the most adventurous man alive.

"At this present time, gentlemen, I am not going to load you with geographical details. The exact spot at which my life ended, in a sense which I presently hope to make clear, can be located at leisure by the proper authorities, to whom I will supply a detailed map which I have in my possession. I am even prepared to guide the expedition, if the Indian Government considers an expedition necessary and cares to accept my services. It's good enough for you to know that pig-sticking and tiger-hunting having begun to pall upon me somewhat, I broke away from Anglo-Indian hospitality, and headed up country, where the Himalayas beckoned. I had figured on crossing at a point where no man has crossed yet, but that project was interrupted, and I'm here to tell you why.

"Up there in the northwest provinces they told me I was crazy when I outlined, one night in a mess, of which I was a guest at the time, my scheme for heading northeast toward a tributary of the Ganges which would bring me to the neighbourhood of Kathmandu, right under the shadow of Everest.

"'Once you leave Kathmandu,' said the mess president, 'you are outside the pale as far as British influence is concerned. I suppose you understand that?'

"I told him I quite understood it.

"'You can't reach Tibet that way,' he said.

"'Never mind, sir,' I answered. 'I can try, if I feel like it.'

"Three days later I set out. I am not superstitious, and if I take a long time to make a plan, once I've made it I generally stick to it. But right at the very beginning of my expedition I had a warning, if ever a man had one. The country through which my route lay is of very curious formation. If you can imagine a section of your own west country viewed through a giant magnifying glass, you have some sort of picture of the territory in which I found myself.

"Gigantic rocks stand up like monstrous tors, or towers, sometimes offering sheer precipices of many hundreds of feet in height. On those sides of these giant tors, however, which are less precipitous, miniature forests are sometimes found, and absolutely impassable jungles.

"Bordering an independent state, this territory is not at all well known, but I had secured as a guide a man named Vadi—or that was the name he gave me whom I knew to be a high-caste Brahmin of good family. He had been with me for some time, and I thought I could trust him. Therefore, once clear of British territory, I took him into my confidence respecting the real object of my journey.

"This was not primarily to scale a peak of the Himalayas, nor even to visit Kathmandu, but to endeavour to obtain a glimpse of the Temple of Fire!

"That has excited your curiosity, gentlemen. I don't suppose any one here has ever heard of the Temple of Fire.

"By some it is regarded as a sort of native legend but it is more than a legend. It is a fact. For seven years I have known it to be a fact, but my tongue has been tied. Listen. Even down in Bombay, the coming of the next great Master is awaited by certain of the natives; and for more than ten years now it has been whispered from end to end of India that he was about to proclaim himself, that disciples moved secretly among the people of every province, and that the unknown teacher in person awaited his hour in a secret temple up near the Tibetan frontier.

"A golden key opens many doors, gentlemen, and at the time of which I am speaking I had obtained more information respecting this secret religion or cult than any other member of the white races had ever collected, or so I thought at the time. I had definite evidence to show that the existence of this man, or demi-god—for by some he was said to possess superhuman powers—was no myth, but an actual fact.

"The collecting of this data was extremely perilous, and one of my informants, with whom I had come in contact while passing through the central provinces, died mysteriously the night before I left Nagpur. I wondered very much on my way north why I was not molested, for I did not fail to see that the death of the man in Nagpur was connected with the fact that he had divulged to me some of the secrets of the religion of Fire-Tongue. Indeed, it was from him that I first learned the name of the high priest of the cult of Fire. Why I was not molested I learned later.

"But to return to Vadi, my Brahmin guide. We had camped for the night in the shadow of one of those giant tors which I have mentioned. The bearers were seated around their fire at some little distance from us, and Vadi and I were consulting respecting our route in the morning, when I decided to take him into my confidence. Accordingly:

"'Vadi,' I said, 'I know for a positive fact that we are within ten miles of the secret Temple of Fire.'

"I shall never forget the look in his eyes, with the reflection of the firelight dancing in them; but he never moved a muscle.

"'The sahib is wise,' he replied.

"'So is Vadi,' said I. 'Therefore he knows how happy a thousand pounds of English money would make him. It is his in return for a sight of the Temple.'

"Still as a carven image, he squatted there watching me, unmoving, expressionless. Then:

"'A man may die for nothing,' he returned, softly. 'Why should the sahib pay a thousand pounds?'

"'Why should the sahib die?' said I.

"'It is forbidden for any to see the Temple, even from a distance.'

"'But if no one ever knows that I have seen it?'

"'Fire-Tongue knows everything,' he replied, and as he pronounced the name, he performed a curious salutation, touching his forefinger with the tip of his tongue, and then laying his hand upon his brow, upon his lips, and upon his breast, at the same time bowing deeply. 'His vengeance is swift and terrible. He wills a man to die, and the man is dead. None save those who have passed through the tests may set eyes upon his temple, nor even speak his name.'

"This conversation took place, as I have already mentioned, in the shadow of one of those strange stone hillocks which abounded here, and it was at this point that I received a warning which might have deterred many men, since it was inexplicable and strangely awesome.

"My attention was drawn to the phenomenon by a sudden cessation of chatter amongst the bearers seated around their fire. I became aware that an absolute stillness had fallen, and in the eyes of the Brahmin who sat facing me I saw a look of exaltation, of wild fanaticism.

"I jerked my head around, looking back over my shoulder, and what I saw I shall never forget, nor to this day have I been able to explain the means by which the illusion was produced.

"Moving downward toward me through the jungle darkness, slowly, evenly, but at a height above the ground of what I judged to be about fifteen feet, was a sort of torch or flambeau, visible because it was faintly luminous; and surmounting it was a darting tongue of blue flame!

"At the moment that I set eyes upon this apparently supernatural spectacle the bearers, crying some word in Hindustani which I did not understand, rose and fled in a body.

"I may say here that I never saw any of them again; although, considering that they took nothing with them, how they regained the nearest village is a mystery which I have never solved.

"Gentlemen, I know the East as few of my fellow-citizens know it. I know something of the powers which are latent in some Orientals and active in others. That my Brahmin guide was a hypnotist and an illusionist, I have since thought.

"For, even as the pattering footsteps of the bearers grew faint in the distance, the fiery torch disappeared as if by magic, and a silken cord was about my throat!

"As I began a desperate fight for life, I realized that, whatever else Vadi might be, he was certainly an expert thug. The jungle, the rocks, seemed to swim around me as I crashed to the ground and felt the Brahmin's knee in the small of my back."

XXXI

STORY OF THE CITY OF FIRE (CONTINUED)

"HOW I MANAGED to think of any defense against such an attack, and especially in the circumstances, is a matter I have often wondered about since. How, having thought of it, I succeeded in putting it into execution, is probably more wonderful still. But I will just state what happened.

"You may observe that I have large hands. Their size and strength served me well on this occasion At the moment that the rope tightened about my throat I reached up and grasped the Brahmin's left thumb. Desperation gave me additional strength, and I snapped it like a stick of candy.

"Just in the nick of time I felt the cord relax, and, although the veins in my head seemed to be bursting, I managed to get my fingers under that damnable rope. To this very hour I can hear Vadi's shriek of pain as I broke his thumb, and it brings the whole scene back to me.

"Clutching the rope with my left hand, I groaned and lay still. The Brahmin slightly shifted his position, which was what I wanted him to do. The brief respite had been sufficient. As he moved, I managed to draw my knees up, very slightly, for he was a big, heavy man, but sufficiently to enable me to throw him off and roll over.

"Then, gentlemen, I dealt with him as he had meant to deal with me; only I used my bare hands and made a job of it.

"I stood up, breathing heavily, and looked down at him where he lay in the shadows at my feet. Dusk had come with a million stars, and almost above my head were flowering creepers festooned from bough to bough. The two campfires danced up and cast their red light upon the jagged rocks of the hillock, which started up from the very heart of the thicket, to stand out like some giant pyramid against the newly risen moon.

"There were night things on the wing, and strange whispering sounds came from the forests clothing the hills. Then came a distant, hollow booming like the sound of artillery, which echoed down the mountain gorges and seemed to roll away over the lowland swamps and die, inaudible, by the remote river. Yet I stood still, looking down at the dead man at my feet. For this strange, mysterious artillery was a phenomenon I had already met with on this fateful march—weird enough and inexplicable, but no novelty to me, for I had previously met with it in the Shan Hills of Burma.

"I was thinking rapidly. It was clear enough now why I had hitherto been unmolested. To Vadi the task had been allotted by the mysterious organization of which he was a member, of removing me quietly and decently, under circumstances which would lead to no official inquiry. Although only animals, insects, and reptiles seemed to be awake about me, yet I could not get rid of the idea that I was watched.

"I remembered the phantom light, and that memory was an unpleasant one. For ten minutes or more I stood there watching and listening, but nothing molested me, nothing human approached. With a rifle resting across my knees, I sat down in the entrance to my tent to await the dawn.

"Later in the night, those phantom guns boomed out again, and again their booming died away in the far valleys. The fires burned lower and lower, but I made no attempt to replenish them; and because I sat there so silent, all kinds of jungle creatures crept furtively out of the shadows and watched me with their glittering eyes. Once a snake crossed almost at my feet, and once some large creature of the cat species, possibly a puma, showed like a silhouette upon the rocky slopes above.

"So the night passed, and dawn found me still sitting there, the dead man huddled on the ground not three paces from me. I am a man who as a rule thinks slowly, but when the light came my mind was fully made up.

"From the man who had died in Nagpur I had learned more about the location of the City of Fire than I had confided to Vadi. In fact, I thought I could undertake to find the way. Upon the most important point of all, however, I had no information: that is to say, I had no idea how to obtain entrance to the place; for I had been given to understand that the way in was a secret known only to the initiated.

"Nevertheless, I had no intention of turning back; and, although I realized that from this point onward I must largely trust to luck, I had no intention of taking unnecessary chances. Accordingly, I dressed myself in Vadi's clothes, and, being very tanned at this time, I think I made a fairly creditable native.

"Faintly throughout the night, above the other sounds of the jungle, I had heard that of distant falling water. Now, my informant at Nagpur, in speaking of the secret temple, had used the words:

"'Whoever would see the fire must quit air and pass through water.'

"This mysterious formula he had firmly declined to translate into comprehensible English; but during my journey I had been considering it from every angle, and I had recently come to the conclusion that the entrance to this mysterious place was in some way concealed by water. Recollecting the gallery under Niagara Falls, I wondered if some similar natural formation was to be looked for here.

"Now, in the light of the morning sun, looking around me from the little plateau upon which I stood, and remembering a vague description of the country which had been given to me, I decided that I was indeed in the neighbourhood of the Temple of Fire.

"We had followed a fairly well-defined path right to this plateau, and that it was nothing less than the high road to the citadel of Fire-Tongue, I no longer doubted. Beneath me stretched a panorama limned in feverish greens and unhealthy yellows. Scarlike rocks triated the jungle clothing the foothills, and through the dancing air, viewed from the arid heights, they had the appearance of running water.

"Swamps to the southeast showed like unhealing wounds upon the face of the landscape. Beyond them spread the lower river waters, the bank of the stream proper being discernible only by reason of a greater greenness in the palm-tops. Venomous green slopes beyond them again, a fringe of dwarf forest, and the brazen skyline.

"On the right, and above me yet, the path entered a district of volcanic rocks, gnarled, twisted, and contorted as with the agonies of some mighty plague which in a forgotten past had seized on the very bowels of the world and had contorted whole mountains and laid waste vast forests and endless plains. Above, the sun, growing hourly more cruel; ahead, more plague-twisted rocks and the scars dancing like running water; and all around the swooning stillness of the tropics.

"The night sounds of the jungle had ceased, giving place to the ceaseless humming of insects. North, south, east, and west lay that haze of heat, like a moving mantle clothing hills and valleys. The sound of falling water remained perceptible.

"And now, gentlemen, I must relate a discovery which I had made in the act of removing Vadi's clothing. Upon his right forearm was branded a mark resembling the apparition which I had witnessed in the night, namely, a little torch, or flambeau, surmounted by a tongue of fire. Even in the light of the morning, amid that oppressive stillness, I could scarcely believe in my own safety, for that to Vadi the duty of assassinating me had been assigned by this ever-watchful, secret organization, whose stronghold I had dared to approach, was a fact beyond dispute.

"Since I seemed to be quite alone on the plateau, I could only suppose that the issue had been regarded as definitely settled, that no doubt had been entertained by Vadi's instructors respecting his success. The plateau upon which I stood was one of a series of giant steps, and on the west was a sheer descent to a dense jungle, where banks of rotten vegetation, sun-dried upon the top, lay heaped about the tree stems.

"Dragging the heavy body of Vadi to the brink of this precipice, I toppled it over, swaying dizzily as I watched it crash down into the poisonous undergrowth two hundred feet below.

"I made a rough cache, where I stored the bulk of my provisions; and, selecting only such articles as I thought necessary for my purpose, I set out again northward, guided by the sound of falling water, and having my face turned toward the silver pencillings in the blue sky, which marked the giant peaks of the distant mountains.

"At midday the heat grew so great that a halt became imperative. The path was still clearly discernible; and in a little cave beside it, which afforded grateful shelter from the merciless rays of the sun, I unfastened my bundle and prepared to take a frugal lunch.

"I was so employed, gentlemen, when I heard the sound of approaching footsteps on the path behind me—the path which I had recently traversed.

"Hastily concealing my bundle, I slipped into some dense undergrowth by the entrance to the cave, and crouched there, waiting and watching. I had not waited very long before a yellow-robed mendicant passed by, carrying a bundle not unlike my own, whereby I concluded that he had come some distance. There was nothing remarkable in his appearance except the fact of his travelling during the hottest part of the day. Therefore I did not doubt that he was one of the members of the secret organization and was bound for headquarters.

"I gave him half an hour's start and then resumed my march. If he could travel beneath a noonday sun, so could I.

"In this fashion I presently came out upon a larger and higher plateau, carpeted with a uniform, stunted undergrowth, and extending, as flat as a table, to the very edge of a sheer precipice, which rose from it to a height of three or four hundred feet—gnarled, naked rock, showing no vestige of vegetation.

"By this time the sound of falling water had become very loud, and as I emerged from the gorge through which the path ran on to this plateau I saw, on the further side of this tableland, the yellow robe of the mendicant. He was walking straight for the face of the precipice, and straight for the spot at which, from a fissure in the rock, a little stream leapt out, to fall sheerly ten or fifteen feet into a winding channel, along which it bubbled away westward, doubtless to form a greater waterfall beyond.

"The mendicant was fully half a mile away from me, but in that clear tropical air was plainly visible; and, fearing that he might look around, I stepped back into the comparative shadow of the gorge and watched.

"Gentlemen, I saw a strange thing. Placing his bundle upon his head, he walked squarely into the face of the waterfall and disappeared!"

XXXII

STORY OF THE CITY OF FIRE (CONTINUED)

"'QUITTING AIR, must pass through water.' The meaning of those words became apparent enough. I stood at the foot of the waterfall, looking up at the fissure from which it issued.

"Although the fact had been most artistically disguised, I could not doubt that this fissure was artificial. A tunnel had been hewn through the rock, and a mountain stream diverted into it. Indeed, on close inspection, I saw that it was little more than a thin curtain of water, partly concealing what looked like the entrance of a cave.

"A great deal of mist arose from it. But I could see that, beyond a ducking, I had little to fear; and, stepping down into the bed of the little stream which frothed and bubbled pleasantly about my bare legs, I set my bundle on my head as the mendicant had done, and plunged through the waterfall, into a place of delicious coolness.

"A strange greenish light prevailed here and directly before me I saw a flight of stone steps leading upward through a tunnel in the rock. By the light of a pocket torch with which I had provided myself, I began to ascend the steps. These, as I have said, were hewn out of the solid rock, and as they numbered something like seven hundred, the labour expended upon the making of this extraordinary staircase must have been stupendous.

"At first the character of the surrounding tunnel suggested that it was, in part at least, a natural cavern. But as I mounted higher and higher, solid masonry appeared in places, some of it displaying unusual carvings, of a character with which I was quite unfamiliar. I concluded that it was very ancient.

"I should explain, gentlemen, that this ascending tunnel zigzagged in a peculiar fashion, which may have been due to the natural formation of the volcanic rock, or may have been part of the design of the original builder. I had ascended more than five hundred steps, and felt that a rest would shortly be necessary, when I reached a sort of cavern, or interior platform, from which seven corridors branched out like the spokes of a wheel. The top of this place was lost in shadows, which the ray of my torch failed to penetrate; and here I paused, setting down my bundle and wondering what my next move should be.

"To the damp coolness of the lower stairs an oppressive heat had now succeeded, and I became aware of a continuous roaring sound, which I found myself unable to explain.

"Attached to a belt beneath my native dress I carried a Colt revolver; and therefore, leaving my rifle and bundle in a corner of the cavern, I selected one of these corridors more or less at random, and set out to explore. This corridor proved to slope very gently upward from the platform, and I could not fail to notice that at every step the heat grew greater and greater. A suffocating, sulphurous smell became perceptible also, and the roaring sound grew almost deafening. It became possible to discern the walls of the corridor ahead because of a sort of eerie bluish light which had now become visible.

"Gentlemen, I don't say that I hesitated in a physical sense: I went right on walking ahead. But a voice somewhere deep down inside me was whispering that this was the road to hell.

"At a point where the heat and the smell were almost unendurable the corridor was blocked by massive iron bars beyond which the reflection of some gigantic fire danced upon the walls of a vast cavern.

"The heat was so great that my garments, saturated by the curtain of water through which I had passed, were now bone dry, and I stood peering through those bars at a spectacle which will remain with me to the merciful day of my death.

"A hundred feet beneath me was a lake of fire! That is the only way I can describe it: a seething, bubbling lake of fire. And above, where the roof of the cavern formed a natural cone, was a square section formed of massive stone blocks, and quite obviously the handiwork of man. The bars were too hot to touch, and the heat was like that of a furnace, but while I stood, peering first upward and then downward, a thing happened which I almost hesitate to describe, for it sounds like an incident from a nightmare.

"Heralded by a rumbling sound which was perceptible above the roar of the fire below, the centre block in the roof slid open. A tremendous draught of air swept along the passage in which I was standing, and doubtless along other passages which opened upon this hell-pit.

"As if conjured up by magic, a monstrous column of blue flame arose, swept up scorchingly, and licked like the tongue of a hungry dragon upon the roof of the cavern. Instantly the trap was closed again; the tongue of fire dropped back into the lake from which it had arisen on the draught of air.

"And right past me where I stood, rigid with horror, looking through those bars, fell a white-robed figure—whether man or woman I could not determine! Down, down into the fiery pit, a hundred feet below!

"One long-drawn, dying shriek reached my ears.

"Of my return to the place at which I had left my bundle and rifle I retain absolutely not one recollection. I was aroused from a sort of stupor of horror by the sight of a faint light moving across the platform ahead of me, as I was about to emerge from the tunnel.

"It was the light of a lantern, carried by a man who might have been the double of that yellow-robed mendicant who had first unconsciously led me to this accursed place.

"I won't deny that, up to the moment of sighting him, my one idea had been to escape, to return, to quit this unholy spot. But now, as I watched the bearer of the lantern cross the platform and enter one of the seven corridors, that old, unquenchable thirst for new experiences got me by the throat again.

"As the light of the lantern was swallowed up in the passage, I found my bundle and rifle and set out to follow the man. Four paces brought me to the foot of more steps. I walked barefooted, frequently pausing to listen. There were many carvings upon the walls, but I had no leisure to examine them.

"Contrary to my anticipations, however, there were no branches in this zigzag staircase, which communicated directly with the top of the lofty plateau. When presently I felt the fresh mountain air upon my face, I wondered why I could perceive no light ahead of me. Yet the reason was simple enough.

"Since I had passed through that strange watergate to the City of Fire, the day had ended: it was night. And when, finding no further steps ahead of me, I passed along a level, narrow corridor for some ten paces and, looking upward, saw the stars, I was astounded.

"The yellow-robed man had disappeared, and I stood alone, looking down upon that secret city which I had come so far to see.

"I found myself standing in deep undergrowth, and, pressing this gently aside, I saw a wonderful spectacle. Away to my left was a great white marble building, which I judged to be a temple; and forming a crescent before it was a miniature town, each white-walled house surrounded by a garden. It was Damascus reduced to fairy dimensions, a spectacle quite unforgettable.

"The fact which made the whole thing awesome and unreal was the presence, along the top of the temple (which, like that of Hatshepsu at Deir elBahari, seemed to be hewn out of the living rock but was faced with white marble) of seven giant flambeaux, each surmounted by a darting tongue of blue flame!

"Legend had it that this was the temple built by Zoroaster and preserved intact by that wonderful secretiveness of the Orient through the generations, by a cult who awaited the coming of Zoroaster's successor, of that Fire-Tongue who was to redeem and revolutionize the world.

"I was afraid to move too far from the mouth of the tunnel, but nevertheless was anxious to obtain a good view of the little city at my feet. Gingerly I moved farther forward and forward, ever craning out for a glimpse of the buildings more immediately below me, forgetful of the fact that I walked upon the brink of a precipice.

"Suddenly my outstretched foot failed to touch ground. I clutched wildly at the bushes around me. Their roots were not firm in the shallow soil, and, enveloped like some pagan god in a mass of foliage, I toppled over the cliff and fell!"

XXXIII

STORY OF THE CITY OF FIRE (CONTINUED)

"MY AWAKENING WAS as strange as anything which had befallen me. I lay upon a silken bed in a pavilion which was furnished with exquisite, if somewhat barbaric, taste.

"A silken shaded lamp hung upon a golden chain near to my couch, but it was dimmed by the rosy light streaming in through the open door—a light which I believed to be that of dawn. I ached in every limb and felt weak and ill. There was a bandage about my head, too, but this great physical weakness numbed my curiosity, and I just lay still, looking out through the doorway into a lovely garden. I could form no impression of what had happened, and the ceaseless throbbing in my head rendered any attempt to do so very painful.

"I was lying there, in this curious and apathetic state, when the curtains draped in the doorway were pulled more widely aside and a woman came in.

"Gentlemen, I will not endeavour to describe her, except to say that she was so darkly lovely that I doubted the evidence of my senses; tall and lithe, with the grace of some beautiful jungle creature.

"When she saw that I was awake, she paused and lowered her head in confusion. She wore a gossamer robe of sheeny golden silk, and, standing there with the light of the dawn behind her, she made a picture that I think would have driven a painter crazy.

"I am supposed to be an unimpressionable man, and perhaps it is true; but there at that moment, as the glance of her dark eyes met the wondering look in mine, I knew that my hour had come for good or ill.

"This is not the time nor the place for personal reminiscences. I am here for another purpose. One of those accidents which are really due to the hand of fate had precipitated me into the garden of the house of Naida, and she in her great compassion had tended me and sheltered me, keeping my presence secret from those who would have dealt with me in summary fashion, and, indeed, who were actually on the look-out for my arrival.

"Yes, so Naida informed me. To my great surprise she spoke almost perfect English, and that sort of understanding sprang up between us immediately which, in the case of a man and a beautiful woman thrown together as we were, can only terminate in one way.

"She was some sort of priestess of the temple which I had seen from the top of the cliff. What else she was I very shortly learned.

"In accordance with one of the many strange customs of the City of Fire, her personal servants, or rather slaves, were blind mutes!

Gentlemen, I warned you that my story was tough. Doubtless you are beginning to appreciate the fact that I spoke no more than the truth.

"Naida, for such was her name, told me that the Brahmin, Vadi, who had acted as my guide, was one of the followers of the Prophet of Fire, to whom had been given the duty of intercepting me. His failure to report within a certain time had resulted in two of the priests of this strange cult being sent out to obtain information. That these were the yellow-robed mendicants who had passed me in the mountains, I did not doubt.

"Their reports, so Naida informed me, had led to a belief that Vadi had perished with me; but as an extra measure of precaution, that very night—indeed, shortly after I had passed that way—a guard had been set upon the secret entrance. Therefore, even if my strength had permitted, I should have been unable to return by the way I had come.

"But indeed I was as weak as a child, and only to the presence of much foliage upon the acclivity down which I had rolled, and to the fact that I had fallen upon soft soil in a bed of flowers, can I ascribe my having failed to break my neck.

"In this way, gentlemen, I entered upon a brief period of my life at once more sweet and more bitter than any I had known. Next to that strange, invisible prophet whose name was Fire-Tongue, Naida held unquestioned sway in this secret city. Her house was separated from the others, and she travelled to and from the temple in a covered litter. To look upon her, as upon Fire-Tongue himself, was death. Women, I learned, were eligible for admission to this order, and these were initiated by Naida.

"As the days of my strange but delightful captivity wore on, I learned more and more of the weird people who, unseen, surrounded me. There were lodges of the Cult of Fire all over the East, all having power to make initiates and some to pass disciples into the higher grades. Those who aspired to the highest rank in the order, however, were compelled to visit this secret city in the Indian hills.

"Then at last I learned a secret which Naida had for long kept back from me. These followers of the new Zoroaster were polygamists, and she was the first or chief wife of the mysterious personage known as Fire-Tongue. I gathered that others had superseded her, and her lord and master rarely visited this marble house set amid its extensive gardens.

"Her dignities remained, however, and no one had aspired to dethrone her as high priestess of the temple. She evidently knew all the secrets of the organization, and I gathered that she was indispensable to the group who controlled it.

"Respecting Fire-Tongue himself, his origin, his appearance, she was resolutely silent, a second Acte, faithful to the last. That the ends of this cult were not only religious but political, she did not deny, but upon this point she was very reticent. An elaborate system of espionage was established throughout the East, Near and Far, and death was the penalty of any breach of fidelity.

"Respecting the tests to which candidates were put, she spoke with more freedom. Those who, having reached the second grade, aspired to the first, were submitted to three very severe ones, to make trial of their courage, purity, and humility. Failure in any of these trials resulted in instant death, and the final test, the trial by fire, which took place in a subterranean chamber of the great temple, resulted in a candidate whose courage failed him being precipitated into that lake of flame which I have already described—a dreadful form of death, which by accident I had witnessed.

"Gentlemen, realizing what the existence of such an organization meant, what a menace to the peace of the world must lie here, what dreadful things were almost hourly happening about me at behest of this invisible monster known as Fire-Tongue, I yet confess—for I am here to speak the truth—that, although I had now fully recovered my strength, I lingered on in a delicious idleness, which you who hear me must find it hard to understand.

"I have the reputation of being a cold, hard man. So had Antony before he met Cleopatra. But seven years ago, under the Indian moon, I learned tolerance for the human weakness which forgets the world for the smiles of a woman.

"It had to end. Sooner or later, discovery was inevitable. One night I told Naida that I must go. Over the scene that followed I will pass in silence. It needed all the strength of a fairly straight, hard life to help me keep to my decision.

"She understood at last, and consented to release me. But there were obstacles—big ones. The snow on the lower mountain slopes had begun to melt, and the water-gate in the valley by which I had entered was now impassable. As a result, I must use another gate, which opened into a mountain path, but which was always guarded. At first, on hearing this, I gave myself up for lost, but Naida had a plan.

"Removing a bangle which she always wore, she showed me the secret mark of Fire-Tongue branded upon the creamy skin.

"'I will put this mark upon your arm,' she said. 'In no other way can you escape. I will teach you some of the passwords by which the brethren know one another, and if you are ever questioned you will say that you were admitted to the order by the Master of the Bombay Lodge, news of whose death has just reached us.'

"'But,' said I, 'how can I hope to pass for an Oriental?'

"'It does not matter,' Naida replied. 'There are some who are not Orientals among us!'

"Gentlemen, those words staggered me, opening up a possibility which had seemed only shadowy before. But Naida, who had tremendous strength of character, definitely refused to discuss this aspect of the matter, merely assuring me that it was so.

"'Those who have successfully passed the ordeal of fire,' she said, 'are put under a vow of silence for one month, and from moon to moon must speak to no living creature. Therefore, once you bear the mark of the Fiery Tongue, you may safely pass the gate, except that there are certain signs which it is necessary you should know. Afterward, if you should ever be in danger of discovery anywhere in the East, you will remember the passwords, which I shall teach you.'

"So I was branded with the mark of Fire-Tongue, and I spent my last night with Naida learning from her lips the words by which members of this order were enabled to recognize one another. In vain I entreated Naida to accompany me. She would allow herself to love and be loved; but the vows of this singular priesthood were to her inviolable.

"She exacted an oath from me that I would never divulge anything which I had seen or heard in the City of Fire. She urged that I must leave India as quickly as possible. I had already learned that this remote society was closely in touch with the affairs of the outside world. And, because I knew I was leaving my heart behind there in the Indian hills, I recognized that this dreadful parting must be final.

"Therefore I scarcely heeded her when she assured me that, should I ever be in danger because of what had happened, a message in the *Times* of India would reach her. I never intended to insert such a message, gentlemen. I knew that it would need all my strength to close this door which I had opened.

"I will spare you and myself the details of our parting. I passed out from the City of Fire in the darkest hour of the night, through a long winding tunnel, half a mile in length. I had protested to Naida that the secret mark might be painted upon my arm and not branded, but she had assured me that the latter was a necessity, and this now became evident; for, not only three times was it subjected to scrutiny, but by the last of the guards, posted near the outer end of the tunnel, it was tested with some kind of solution.

"Silence and the salutation with the moistened finger tips, together with the brand upon my arm, won me freedom from the abode of Fire-Tongue.

"From a village situated upon one of the tributaries of the Ganges I readily obtained a guide, to whom such silent, yellow-robed figures as mine were evidently not unfamiliar; and, crossing the east of Nepal, I entered Bengal, bearing a strange secret. I found myself in an empty world—a world which had nothing to offer me. For every step south took me farther from all that made life worth living."

XXXIV

NICOL BRINN'S STORY (CONCLUDED)

"THE INCIDENTS OF the next seven years do not concern you, gentlemen. I had one aim in life—to forget. I earned an unenviable reputation for foolhardy enterprises. Until this very hour, no man has known why I did the things that I did do. From the time that I left India until the moment when fate literally threw me in the way of the late Sir Charles Abingdon, I had heard nothing of the cult of Fire-Tongue; and in spite of Naida's assurance that its membership was not confined to Orientals, I had long ago supposed it to be a manifestation of local fanaticism, having no political or international significance.

"Then, lunching with the late Sir Charles after my accident in the Haymarket, he put to me a question which literally made me hold my breath.

"'Do you know anything of the significance of the term Fire-Tongue?' he asked.

"I am not accustomed to any display of feeling in public, and I replied in what I think was an ordinary tone:

"'In what connection, Sir Charles?'

"'Well,' said he, watching me oddly, 'I know you have travelled in India, and I wondered if you had ever come in contact with the legend which prevails there, that a second Zoroaster has arisen, to preach the doctrine of eternal fire.'

"'I have heard it,' I replied, guardedly.

"'I thought it possible,' continued Sir Charles, 'and I am tempted to tell you of a curious experience which once befell me during the time that I was a guest of my late friend Colonel Banfield in Delhi. My reputation as an osteologist was not at that time so fully established as it later became, but I already had some reputation in this branch of surgery; and one evening a very dignified Hindu gentleman sought an interview with me, saying that a distinguished native noble, who was a guest of his, had met with a serious accident, and offering me a fee equivalent to nearly five hundred pounds to perform an operation which he believed to be necessary.

"'I assured him that my services were at his disposal, and blankly declined to accept so large a fee. He thereupon explained that the circumstances were peculiar. His friend belonged to a religious cult of an extremely high order. He would lose caste if it became known that he had been attended by a Christian surgeon; therefore my visit must be a secret one.

"'It made no difference,' I replied. 'I quite understood; and he might rely upon my discretion.

"'Accordingly I was driven in a car which was waiting to some house upon the outskirts of the city and conducted to a room where the patient had been carried. I saw him to be a singularly handsome young man, apparently about twenty-three years of age. His features were flawless, and he possessed light ivory skin and wavy jet-black hair. His eyes, which were very dark and almond-shaped, had a strange and arresting beauty. But there was something effeminate about him which repelled me, I cannot say in what way; nor did I approve of the presence of many bowls of hyacinths in the room.

"'However, I performed the operation, which, although slight, demanded some skill, and with the nature of which I will not trouble you. Intense anxiety was manifested by the young man's attendants, and one of these, a strikingly beautiful woman, insisted on remaining while the operation was performed.

"'She seemed more especially to concern herself with preserving intact a lock of the young man's jet-black hair, which was brushed in rather an odd manner across his ivory forehead. Naturally enough, this circumstance excited my curiosity and, distracting the woman's attention for a moment—I asked her to bring me something from a table at the opposite side of the room—I lightly raised this wayward lock and immediately replaced it again.

"'Do you know what it concealed, Mr. Brinn?'

"I assured him that I did not.

"'A mark, apparently natural, resembling a torch surmounted by a tongue of fire!'

"I was amazed, gentlemen, by Sir Charles's story. He was given his fee and driven back to his quarters But that he had succeeded where I had failed, that he had actually looked upon Fire-Tongue in person, I could not doubt. I learned from this, too, that the Prophet of Fire did not always remain in his mountain stronghold, for Delhi is a long way from the Secret City.

"Strange though it must appear, at this time I failed to account for Sir Charles confiding this thing to me. Later, I realized that he must have seen the mark on my arm, although he never referred to it.

"Well, the past leapt out at me, as you see, and worse was to come. The death of Sir Charles Abingdon told me what I hated to know: that Fire-Tongue was in England!

"I moved at once. I inserted in the *Times* the prearranged message, hardly daring to hope that it would come to the eye of Naida; but it did! She visited me. And I learned that not only Sir Charles Abingdon, but another, knew of the mark which I bore!

"I was summoned to appear before the Prophet of fire!

"Gentlemen, what I saw and how I succeeded in finding out the location of his abode are matters that can wait. The important things are these: first, I learned why Sir Charles Abingdon had been done to death!

"The unwelcome attentions of the man known as Ormuz Khan led Sir Charles to seek an interview with him. I may say here and now that Ormuz Khan is Fire-Tongue! Oh! it's a tough statement—but I can prove it. Sir Charles practically forced his way into this man's presence—and immediately recognized his mysterious patient of years ago!

"He accused him of having set spies upon his daughter's movements—an accusation which was true—and forbade him to see her again. From that hour the fate of Sir Charles was sealed. What he knew, the world must never know. He had recorded, in a private paper, all that he had learned. This paper was stolen from his bureau—and its contents led to my being summoned to the house of Fire-Tongue! It also spurred the organization to renewed efforts, for it revealed the fact that Sir Charles contemplated confiding the story to others.

"What were the intentions of the man Ormuz in regard to Miss Abingdon, I don't know. His entourage all left England some days ago—with three exceptions. I believe him to have been capable of almost anything. He was desperate. He knew that Ormuz Khan must finally and definitely disappear. It is just possible that he meant Miss Abingdon to disappear along with him!

"However, that danger is past. Mrs. McMurdoch, who today accompanied her to his house, was drugged by these past-masters in the use of poisons, and left unconscious in a cottage a few miles from Hillside, the abode of Ormuz.

"You will have observed, gentlemen, that I am somewhat damaged. However, it was worth it! That the organization of the Fire-Worshippers is destroyed I am not prepared to assert. But I made a discovery today which untied my hands. Hearing, I shall never know how, that Naida had had a secret interview with me, Fire-Tongue visited upon her the penalty paid seven years ago by my informant in Nagpur, by Sir Charles Abingdon, recently, by God alone knows how many scores—hundreds—in the history of this damnable group.

"I found her lying on a silken divan in the deserted house, her hands clasped over a little white flower like an odontoglossum, which lay on her breast. It was the flower of sleep—and she was dead.

"My seven years' silence was ended. One thing I could do for the world: remove Fire-Tongue—and do it with my own hands!

"Gentlemen, at the angle where the high road from Upper Claybury joins the Dover Road is the Merton Cottage Hospital. Mr. Harley is awaiting us there. He is less damaged than I am. A native chauffeur, whose name I don't know, is lying insensible in one of the beds—and in another is a dead man, unrecognizable, except for a birthmark resembling a torch on his forehead, his head crushed and his neck broken.

"That dead man is Fire-Tongue. I should like, Mr. Commissioner, to sign the statement."

THE END

Printed in the United States
879000003BA